FOR THE GREATER GLORY OF JAPAN

We were almost to the sixteenth floor when the elevator came to a smooth halt. I picked up my bag and prepared to exit when I realized the operator had not opened the door. The row of lights above the door indicated we were between the fourteenth and fifteenth floors.

"What's going on?" I asked, looking closely at him for the first time.

The operator turned toward me, his face stern, and stood very straight as he pulled a narrow white shawl from his jacket and wrapped it around his neck.

"Death to my enemies," he said quietly in Japanese.

I quickly dropped my suitcase, expecting a lunge from him. Instead he whirled and lifted the emergency phone from its cradle and gave it a yank.

A terrific explosion went off directly above us with a dull compressive blast. The elevator swayed sickeningly for an instant, and then began to fall. . . .

From The Nick Carter Killmaster Series

NC-B

NICK CARTER IS IT!

NC-A

Dedicated to The Men of the
Secret Services of the
United States of America

A Killmaster Spy Chiller

NICK CARTER

THE SIGN
OF THE
PRAYER SHAWL

CHARTER
NEW YORK

A DIVISION OF CHARTER COMMUNICATIONS INC.
A GROSSET & DUNLAP COMPANY

THE SIGN OF THE PRAYER SHAWL

THE SIGN
OF THE
PRAYER SHAWL

CHAPTER ONE

"Pan American flight three-one-three is now arriving at gate G-2. Pan American flight three-one-three. . . ."

The soft but metallic female voice purring from the restaurant intercom caught my attention and I glanced quickly at my watch. That flight was not the one I was meeting, but the announcement reminded me that I could not dawdle any longer over breakfast if I wanted to see Owen's flight come in.

I drank the last of my coffee, stubbed out my cigarette, pushed the plush rollered chair away from the table and raised my hand to signal the waitress for my check.

She glided across the thick pale orange carpet and handed me the ticket with a warm smile. "Hope you enjoyed your meal," she said.

"I did, thanks," I said, looking up at her and returning the smile. I left a generous tip, then rose and took a last look around the pleasant dining room. It felt good to relax between missions and to treat myself to a leisurely meal without worrying about enemy agents watching my every move. I knew that I now looked like one of many trim businessmen in tan suits who came to San Francisco's International Airport in the early morning and dined at ease, only to jump up and rush out at the announcement of a flight.

As I paid the bill the pretty young cashier gave me an appraising once-over with her wide, deep brown eyes and a little smile. But this morning I did not have the time to take her up on her obvious offer, so I merely smiled back and left, feeling her disappointed stare on my back.

Hurrying out into the main mezzanine, I walked briskly toward the Northwest Orient check-in desk. The televi-

sion screen above the counter indicated Flight 721 from
Tokyo and Honolulu was scheduled to arrive at 7:40
A.M. Owen was coming in on one of the DC-10 jumbo jets,
and I wanted to watch the big plane land.

It was already seven-thirty, so I hustled out to the wide
corridor leading to gate K-3, gripping the heavy binocular
case that hung from my shoulder to keep it from
bouncing against me as I half ran and half jogged. My
rapid footsteps echoed in the nearly deserted building as I
hurried past the morning janitorial staff. The bustle of San
Francisco's International had not yet reached its characteristic level of near chaos, and the janitors watched me
pass with indifferent amusement.

The cloudless sky hung like a curtain of azure blue
through the floor to ceiling corridor windows. The
warmly-dressed ground crews outside seemed predisposed
to stand and talk, rather than work, clouds of condensed
moisture blowing out of their mouths with every sleepy-
eyed comment they made. Even the low carts and trailers
carrying baggage seemed to be moving at a sane pace instead of the usual daredevil style seen at airports.

When I reached gate K-3 I went immediately to the
window that overlooked the runways and took out my
fifty-power special issue Zeuss X-111 binoculars. I
scanned the horizon in a series of rapid sweeps but saw
no incoming planes, so I scanned the airport itself and the
surrounding countryside.

Airports had always fascinated me since I was a kid,
and even before becoming AXE Killmaster N3 I knew of
their role in international smuggling and intrigue. I never
lost an opportunity to observe the layout and daily operations of every one in which I happened to find myself.
Tidbits of fact were learned every time I looked around a
hanger, or hung around the gates watching people come
and go. Small bits of data were stored in my brain:
mostly trivial facts, it's true, but the few important items
of information gleaned in this way and recalled at some
crucial moment were more than worth the slight trouble

of careful observation. They could be and had been—on several occasions—life savers. Besides, careful scrutiny is a habit that grows rusty if not constantly used.

It was a wet morning too, and dew sparkled from the flat green lawns that surrounded the few homes I could see from my vantage point. To the north, toward San Francisco itself, the fog was thick on the bay side of the peninsula.

I lowered the field glasses and scanned the sky again with my naked eye. This time I caught the tiny dark speck in the distant blue atmospheric depths. I lifted the binoculars.

The giant DC-10 drifted slowly through the field of my glasses like some metallic predatory bird in a graceful, and from here, silent dive toward prey. The flaps were already lowered and the landing gear was down. I knew the DC-10's wing span was three hundred and forty feet, and from the angular size of the craft in the binocular's visual field, I estimated its distance to be about five miles. At an approach speed of around two hundred miles per hour, it would touch down in less than two minutes. I glanced at my watch and smiled with anticipation. The plane was only a few minutes late; not long to wait for an old friend, I told myself.

Yet the circumstances surrounding Owen's arrival from Tokyo were far from clear to me. In fact, they were very mysterious. Owen had been worried about something when we talked by phone two days ago.

"I'll see you soon, Nick," he had said when our conversation was almost over. That surprised me because I had not expected the Far East resident agent for AXE to travel to the States, nor had I expected to be in Japan at any near date.

"What do you mean, Owen?" I asked.

"I don't have all the pieces of this puzzle yet, or I could tell you more. But it's extremely important, Nick. I can't risk a leak at this stage, so I'll take the next flight out and talk to you in person. Hawk knows about it."

Owen had sounded almost frightened on the phone that day. Frightened not for his personal safety, of course, but frightened nevertheless. And that in itself was odd, because Owen Nashima was one of the most courageous AXE agents I had ever known. His Japanese ancestry had included a healthy amount of Samurai strain, which lent him an absolute fearlessness in hand-to-hand combat known well at the Washington offices of Amalgamated Press and Wire Services, the front organization for AXE, America's most covert and capable espionage agency.

Owen's fear had infected me. Whatever he was working on must be big to warrant a special trip Stateside and a person-to-person meeting.

And when Hawk had sent me the top secret message the day after Owen telephoned, saying that Nashima would arrive the next day in San Francisco, I knew that even AXE's tough-minded Operations Chief was concerned too. Yet Hawk's message to me had contained no clue to what the matter might be all about.

Flight 721 was now in its final glidepath and I watched the aircraft settle into its characteristic nose-up landing posture. Damn, it would be good to see Owen again. Too bad one of my best friends had to be stationed half way around the world.

I couldn't help smiling as I watched the DC-10 descend. Owen was one of the most humorous agents ever to infest AXE, as Hawk had grudgingly phrased it in one of his weaker moments. Nashima had completely integrated the Eastern and Western ways of thinking and feeling, with the result that his outlook on life, his humor and even his approach to AXE operations were unique, and often funny. But his methods were also highly effective, which was why Hawk had entrusted the entire Eastern Region to him.

I had met Owen five years ago while I was on a mission to Japan calling for close cooperation between us. I had been nervous about working with a man I had not had the chance to personally evaluate, and the Americanized dive he chose for us to meet in didn't make me feel any better.

After I had stood at one end of the bar for ten minutes I was approached by a tall Japanese man wearing a classic silk kimono of blue, gold and red, looking like the lead warrior in a Japanese play.

He stepped close and bowed low. "Mister Nick Carter?" His singsong accent was so pronounced I could barely understand my own name.

I nodded suspiciously.

He blurted in rapid-fire Japanese something to the effect that his name was Oshigao Nashima, then bowed deeply again and when he came back up looked deeply and directly into my eyes.

I was still learning Oriental languages and was not yet completely fluent in Japanese. But I had understood enough of what he said to realize that this man was my partner.

I returned his deep gaze impatient to know what the hell was going on. Reading the character of a person from his face and eyes is a skill I pride myself on, and I welcomed the chance to see what kind of a man he was. Yet when I looked into his eyes I was truly shocked. I could see nothing from them. He had turned the most opaque pair of eyes on me that I had ever encountered, and it was disconcerting.

At first I thought it was an example of the inscrutable oriental gaze, yet it quickly became more earnest than that. I found myself locked into his gaze, and for five of the longest seconds in my life, I was transfixed and immobile as his eyes bored into mine and he seemed to read my soul. At last he blinked and looked away for a moment.

Immediately his face became animated and softer, with warmth flowing into his lively brown eyes. He extended his hand and took mine.

"Call me Owen," he said in perfect English, smiling broadly.

We became fast friends during that mission and I

learned more from him than from almost any other agent I have ever worked with. He was a master of Japanese and Chinese dialect and idiom, and of the martial arts and philosophies of the East. And he was an excellent teacher.

It would be good to see him again, and to learn what it was that worried him so much.

The DC-10 was at about one thousand feet and less than a mile from touchdown when it happened. I was about to lower the binoculars when I noticed that the plane was rocking sickeningly as if out of control. It steadied itself, though, and the muted roar of the supressed jet engines suddenly increased to a loud blast as full thrust was poured into the J-18 engines powering the craft. The big plane halted its descent and leveled off, then banked sharply and went into a shallow dive directly toward the main passenger terminal and control tower atop that.

My hands were suddenly wet and slippery on the binoculars as I stood helplessly behind the tinted glass window and watched the gigantic airplane zero in on the control tower. It almost seemed as if the DC-10 were not out of control. It was as if the pilot had suddenly gone berserk and was playing some kind of gruesome game. I could see the flight controllers frantically running back and forth within their elevated prison from which there suddenly was no escape.

The plane dipped as if it would hit the tower broadside, but then it nosed up and clipped off the glass top of the structure. I squinted at the plane's flaps, doors and wings during those few brief seconds, looking for any kind of evidence of structural failure or damage that might account for the monster bird to suddenly go mad. But I saw nothing out of order, and, in a flash of reflected sunlight, the plane went out of sight beyond the building.

A few seconds later I heard an explosive roar and an extended ripping sound, the screech of metal being torn, of bolts and struts being pulled apart by superhuman forces. As I turned from the windows and raced back along the corridor, the sounds of the crash died slowly and a single, horrendous explosion followed. It must have been the fuel tanks, I thought, as I sprinted across the terminal floor and took the stairs to the second level.

I did not have to search the horizon to see where the DC-10 had come down. It had missed the freeway and the few warehouses adjacent to the airport, and had plowed through dozens of houses covering the rolling hills to the east. From my vantage point it looked as if several city blocks had been annihilated.

Sirens began to wail and official-looking people ran through the terminal as I went back downstairs. My footsteps beat hard and sharp on the polished floor as I sprinted to the doors and hailed a cab outside.

I jumped into the taxi before it came to a stop. "A friend of mine was in that crash," I shouted. "There's twenty bucks for you if you get me there fast."

The cabby snatched the bill and jerked the car into the traffic. "We'll be the first ones there, buddy," he said.

We arrived with the firetrucks and ambulances. The scene looked as if a tornado had gone through and smashed house after house into fragments of white pine and colored shingles. Brown earth was plowed up and turned onto the green lawns. Slender threads of blue smoke were rising already from the rubble, and a single thick black column lifted skyward from the burning rubber tire.

The cabby drove up a slight hill along the street parallel to the crash path until he reached the end of the destruction, where the airplane had come to a rest. What was left of it, that is. Only the tail section remained intact, and there were no seats visible in the hollow metal shell.

As I slammed the car door and stepped toward the rubble, an irritating odor of burning kerosene struck me full in the nostrils. I coughed involuntarily and breathed less deeply to avoid taking in too much of the chemical. The fuel vapors were wafting my way from a jet engine laying in a backyard about fifty feet upwind. The huge powerhouse torn loose from the tail section had come to rest beside a small white doghouse behind a miraculously undamaged house.

Looking downhill, I could see fragments of the fuselage scattered along the path of destruction. Bodies were strewn here and there; some of them intact, others ripped apart by the violent impact and deceleration. Some were still strapped to their seats that had come loose from the cabin floor.

As I stood desperately wondering where to begin looking for Owen, I became aware of an eerie silence that had spread over the awful landscape. It was almost a sorrowful moment of solitude; as if some supernatural power were observing and mourning the carnage.

Then the screams began. Low moans at first as the survivors came out of their shock and felt the searing pain in their limbs and guts, and shortly thereafter came the loud incoherent cries as those damaged souls tried to question and make sense of the event that had suddenly shattered lives.

My rescue reflexes came into play and I stumbled over the rubble to where the calls were the loudest. I stopped near a pair of upside-down seats. In one of them was strapped a middle-aged woman, slender and pretty, while in the other a young boy was twisted around and was pushing against the earth under him.

He coughed and shook his head spasmodically, then lay quietly as I pulled the seats upright and laid them on their backs. The boy was suddenly too quiet.

I bent over him and saw that he was in shock and had quit breathing. I gripped his jaw and forced open his mouth, saw that his tongue was clear of his throat, then took a deep breath and put my mouth over his, closing his nostrils with my free hand. His chest rose as I exhaled forcefully into his mouth. By my third or fourth breath he sputtered and pushed me away, and began to breathe on his own.

I looked around to see that the ambulance attendants

were carrying stretchers among the wreckage and looking for survivors. I stood up and snapped off a loud command. "Medic! This one can be saved."

They immediately rushed our way, and after glancing down at the woman strapped into the seat next to the boy, I went to search for other survivors. Her neck had been broken, and her jugular vein torn half out of her throat.

I would have preferred to confine my search for Owen, but the emergency demanded that as many as possible be saved, so I continued to help in the rescue operation and hoped against hope that Owen Nashima might be among those still alive.

More ambulances were beginning to arrive now, and neighborhood residents were arriving to help with the rescue work. The sun rose higher with the hours and the day warmed. Miles to the north, the fog lifted from the bay area, and it seemed oddly incongruous that such a nice day could be coming amid this death and destruction.

As I loaded bodies onto stretchers, I could not shake the feeling that somehow this crash was not an accident. I was certain it was related to the secret Owen had discovered and told no one about; a secret so important that hundreds of innocent people had been killed to keep one man from telling it. And I also had a dull ache in my gut; the fear that my friend would not be found alive.

CHAPTER TWO

"I'm sorry, Mr. Carter, but Mr. Tsumoto did die in the crash." The young Federal Aviation Administration Information Officer looked sympathetically up from the clipboard that listed the fate of each passenger aboard Northwest Orient Flight 721.

My face must have shown the sorrow I felt, because he added softly, "Were you close to him?"

"Yes," I said slowly. "Tataka Tsumoto and I were the closest of friends." Owen had flown under the cover name of Tsumoto and I was one of the few people in the world who knew the real identity of the person now dead under that borrowed name.

The FAA investigative team had temporarily taken over a section of Northwest Orient's ticket area at San Francisco International in order to have an information center to handle inquiries by relatives of the crash victims.

I leaned on one elbow on the off-white formica counter. "Were any of his things salvaged from the wreckage?" I asked. "Any papers?"

The officer checked another clipboard. "His baggage was lost," he said. "Burned, probably. But his wallet and personal effects have been collected." His manner became more businesslike. "They'll be sent to his next of kin."

I nodded. Owen wouldn't have left clues among anything he carried on his person, so I did not think it would be worthwhile to get possession of his things. Any important papers he might have been carrying would have been locked in his special briefcase. If the case had been tampered with, or banged up in the crash, all the papers inside would have been immediately burned up with an incinderary device. Neat and very effective.

"What caused the crash?" I asked, changing my tack. "Any word on it yet?"

"Our investigation is still under way, Mr. Carter," he said. "We have not released anything yet to the press. You can look for a story in the newspapers within the next few days."

"But you've already had two days," I insisted, my emotional state obvious in my voice.

He shrugged. "I'm sorry. We're proceeding as fast as possible under the circumstances."

I reached into a pocket and removed a package of my custom-made Turkish cigarettes, extracted one and pretended to study the gold embossed initials N.C. on the filter. I was more familiar than he was with those thousands of bits and pieces of DC-10 scattered across acres of plowed up suburban lawns and demolished houses. I had spent most of the previous two days going over the area looking for some clues about the crash, having used a FBI cover identity to gain access to the crash site. In the confusion I had not been able to find out anything about Owen until this moment, but I had heard enough on-site conversations among the bomb experts and FAA inspectors to learn that there was no explosion aboard the aircraft. The crash was still a matter of conjecture.

"What about the flight recorder?" I asked the officer after a long moment. If anything would shed light on the mishap, that fireproof metal box would. It contained a small but capable tape unit that continuously recorded radio transmissions, cockpit talk and noises as well as the flight status of all crucial systems of the DC-10 such as engine thrust settings, flap positions and fuel levels. Flight recorders were often the FAA's last resort in particularly bad crashes when a plane was totally destroyed.

The information officer opened his mouth to answer, but hesitated as he looked behind me.

Suddenly I was elbowed aside, not too gently, by a frantic young Japanese man dressed in baggy slacks and a loose fitting blue ski jacket. He interrupted without apology and addressed the officer in a tense, excited voice.

"I am Higashi Tsumoto," he said in English with a strong Japanese accent. "My cousin was to arrive on the plane that crashed." He paused with a catch in his voice. "Was he injured?"

He glanced at me with frightened eyes, and gestured helplessly at the officer. "His name is Tataka Tsumoto."

The information officer studied him for a moment, then seemed to forgive his rude intrusion. "There was a Tataka Tsumoto on the flight," he said. "He died in the accident, I'm sorry to say."

The Japanese man bowed his head and squeezed his eyes tightly shut. "This will be very difficult for his mother," he mumbled. Then he straightened up with a look of resolution in his face. "I must return home to tell his family. Are there any possessions I can deliver to them?"

The information officer glanced around to another official who sat at a desk. The second officer had been listening to the conversation and he rose and approached the counter.

"If you can show us some identification, Mr. Tsumoto, and sign the release forms, I think we could give his personal effects to you."

"Of course," the man nodded.

"If you will step this way please, sir," the officer said. He led the Japanese man around the counter to a desk where he had the man sign a number of forms. Then the officer went through a door into the back rooms.

I stood there wondering what the hell was going on, because Tataka Tsumoto was a cover name supposedly known only to AXE personnel. Either this so-called cousin was involved with AXE—which was doubtful—or else a leak had revealed Owen's cover to others. Either way something was wrong here. And the crash itself was beginning to seem less and less like a horrible accident to me.

I motioned to the information officer who returned to where I was standing.

"What about the flight recorder?" I repeated my earlier question. "Did it indicate any flight difficulties before the crash?"

"It's been sent to Washington," he replied curtly as if he thought the mention of that city would satisfy me.

I nodded and inhaled deeply on my cigarette, but my curiosity was only heightened by his admission. I knew that flight recorders were usually kept at the scene of the FAA investigation, at least initially. "Isn't that a little unusual, this early in the investigation?" I asked.

"No," he said. "It's standard operating procedure." He looked anxious to get back to whatever it was that would take him away from my questions.

The other officer returned and set a small cardboard box down on the desk, and handed Tsumoto's "cousin" another form to sign.

The Japanese man signed the last form, got up and tucked the carton under one arm, then surprised me by turning my way. "I heard you say you were Tataka's friend," he said. He hesitated a moment, then offered his hand, shaking mine with a grave formality.

"It is a sad occasion," I said, bowing slightly to him. His appearance was modern enough, yet there was something anachronistic about his manner. He had bowed sharply with a certain stiffness that stamped him as a traditional Japanese; not as Americanized as his clothes might suggest. "It is difficult to lose a cousin," I offered after an uncomfortable silence.

He sighed, then spoke solemnly. "We went to school together here."

School in San Francisco? I knew Owen Nashima had lived in San Francisco during part of his school years, a period when his father was globe-hopping in pursuit of his import-export business, and taking his first child and only son with him.

But we were not talking about Owen Nashima; we were

talking about a cover identity named Tsumoto—a fictional character. Or were we?

Owen's father had been a renegade from his family and had caused a furor among his brothers-in-law when he deserted Japan just before the beginning of World War II, and came to the United States. The family rift was great, with Owen and his father at odds with Owen's mother and sister as well as with his uncles. But the family was patched together late, as I recalled. And although they were never close after the war, at least they all seemed to be on speaking terms.

Owen's strong attachment for his father led him to acquire a taste for global intrigue and experience, traits that eventually suited him for service in AXE.

But what would this Tsumoto imposter know about Owen Nashima, I wondered? I was confused about a lot of things, so I decided to play along with him to see what he was up to.

"How is Tataka's father?" I asked. "Is his business doing well?"

He brightened measurably at the question. "The import business has never been better," he said. "Tataka's mother and sister are well also."

What I was hearing was becoming more and more strange with each exchange. Owen Nashima's father was still an importer, and he did have only one sister. The man in front of me talking about a Tataka Tsumoto was describing Owen Nashima's family to perfection.

I found myself being forced to play along with this man. Somewhere there was a clue of some kind. Was he trying to force my hand? And how much did he actually know about Owen, his cover identity, the crash of the airplane, and—more importantly—the secret Owen had been working on before he was killed? I had to find the answers to those questions.

The cousin seemed anxious to leave now, but before he did he asked me a final surprising question. "Would you like to join me for a drink tonight and spend a little time remembering our mutual friend?"

"I'd be delighted," I said in a properly subdued manner. His invitation was obviously some kind of a trap, but one that I was going to walk into with both eyes open.

"I'll meet you at the Chinaman's Hat at eight?" he asked. "Are you familiar with Chinatown?"

"I can find the place," I replied.

He nodded and bowed again, then turned and rushed away.

My first instinct was to follow the man, but then I decided against it. If he was involved in this business, he would show up at eight tonight as promised. And, meanwhile, I did not want to reveal my position or interest by following him. If he spotted me, what little cover I had left would be blown.

It was just eight o'clock by the time I had walked Chinatown's narrow streets, passing dozens of small, hole-in-the-wall Oriental shops with their glowing paper globes and delicately painted signs, and I was more depressed than I had been in a long time. The bar in the Chinaman's Hat made me nostalgic for the last days with Owen in Tokyo when we matched up with a pair of interesting women and closed several bars in the early morning hours.

It was the mood in the Chinaman's Hat that made me even more depressed: soft strains of Eastern music and dim lights from paper lanterns made me naturally think of Owen.

I had chosen a barstool at one end and had settled down to a brandy Manhattan when Higashi Tsumoto slipped onto the stool next to mine and ordered a sake. He wore a nicely tailored brown suit and this evening managed to look much more Americanized than he had this afternoon at the airport. He gulped the drink silently and quickly despite it being steaming hot. Finally he turned to me and opened the conversation.

"How did you know Tataka?"

"We met during a business deal in Tokyo several years ago," I said.

"Are you in newspaper work as well?" he asked.

I shook my head. "Trading. Oriental furniture."

"I see," he said. "I thought you might be a writer." He stopped a moment to order another round for us, then looked at me again with his appraising eyes. "Tataka has been an editor for several years."

I sipped my drink to hide the shock I was feeling at the moment. This man knew entirely too much about AXE business and about Owen's background. But what was he doing with this information? And what did he want from me?

"Was Tataka still with the same outfit, the . . . the. . . ," I said, trailing off, letting him have the opening.

"Amalgamated Press?" he said. "Yes, he was."

That was AXE's front, and it was supposedly a closely guarded secret. Whoever this man was he was either a fool or a very dangerous adversary. But whatever he was, he was playing a cat and mouse game with me now.

Tsumoto finished his second drink and clicked the small cup onto the bar with a sharp thrust of his hand, then stared silently at me for a moment. "I'm very unhappy with poor Tataka's fate," he said almost melodramatically. "I think a Chinese bath would help. Would you care to join me?"

"It's been years since I've permitted myself that pleasure," I said, stepping down from the bar. "I'd be happy to join you."

We left the Chinaman's Hat and walked a few blocks to a large building constructed in Oriental style, with heavy beams of dark wood supporting a pagoda-like roof whose sweeping corners reached high into the black night. Passing through a minature garden, we found the entrance and a small gracefully carved sign that identified the establishment as the Oriental Fare. Although no one had followed us from the bar, I was sure I was being set up, and every one of my senses were heightened waiting for the smallest clue.

Inside, we were greeted by a young, tuxedoed Oriental man who smiled enthusiastically from behind a registration desk.

"What may I offer you gentlemen this evening for entertainment?" he said, his greeting a mixture of American come-on and Eastern subtlety.

"Massage and bath," Tsumoto said.

The host nodded and turned to the pigeonholes behind him, retrieving two wooden slats covered with bright yellow Chinese symbols. "That will be fifty dollars each," he said, pushing the wooden tickets across the counter.

We paid and took the stairs to the second floor, arriving at one end of a long corridor whose soft yellow walls were covered with delicate Oriental sketches. A diminutive Chinese madam emerged from the first door to our right and stopped us with a friendly smile. She carried two pairs of slippers which she indicated silently we were to wear, and after storing our shoes, jackets, shirts and ties, took our tokens and led us down the hall.

The distant sounds of Eastern stringed instruments helped create an illusion that we were gliding through a sunset-yellow evening sky among willow trees in a Chinese countryside. Vivid images of my past visits to that part of the world swept out of my memory and whirled around in my mind as we progressed to the door where she stopped and bade us enter with a sweep of her arm.

We stepped into a small room fashioned in the Oriental style of simplicity and grace. The walls were soft blue and a faint aroma of sandlewood incense was in the air. A low table set with cups and linen napkins stood to one side, surrounded by dark blue cushions.

As the door was shut softly behind us, two strikingly beautiful women in their mid-twenties stepped from be-

hind a white rice-paper partition and bowed briefly.
Though neither of them was Oriental, they were as exotic
as the atmosphere in the room. The taller of the women
was a slender Polynesian with full lips, wide dark eyes
and sleek black hair. She introduced herself as Lia. The
other, a Philippine beauty named Naomi, was shorter but
no less attractive. Her dark, intense features gave her an
air of mystery.

They both wore plain, tight-fitting linen dresses with
purple trim around the high neck and a split up one side
of the skirt revealing a wide expanse of thigh. Although
both women greeted us with subdued smiles and a com-
fortable ease, I noted a bright look of appreciation in
their eyes. We were not the usual fare of chubby, half-
drunk men skipping the happy hour at some convention
to get a quick piece of the massage action.

"Would you gentlemen care for some tea?" asked Lia.

I was about to accept when Tsumoto cut in curtly.
"Massage and bath first, then tea," he said.

He looked at me and I nodded to indicate that I would
honor the wish of my boorish companion. Lia and Naomi
bowed and led us past the white partition into a large
square room containing two massage couches and a tiled
bath about the size of a king-sized bed. The walls were
pale gold with red trim, and the floor was carpeted in yellow. A frightening beast in gold and red was painted on
the wall near the bath, and its image was reflected in the
dim light from a series of mirrors over each couch.

The women indicated we could undress behind separate
partitions, and I was grateful for the chance to disrobe
without revealing my 9 mm Auger, Wilhelmina, or my
stiletto, Hugo. I had left my gas bomb at my hotel room
for the evening because I had not expected any large-
scale trouble.

I chose a purple towel from a stack of them and
wrapped it around my waist, stepping out from behind
the partition just as Tsumoto did. From the looks Lia and
Naomi gave us, we might have been Olympian gods. My

own physical condition had been kept razor-sharp for
years by hard physical exercise and a yearly stint of train-
ing with special AXE physical fitness instructors. But I
was surprised to see that Tsumoto was in much the same
condition. His clothing had hidden the size of his arms
and shoulders, and kept me from realizing until now that
although half a head shorter, Tsumoto was probably
stronger than I was.

"Please come this way and lie down," Lia said. As we
were stretching out on the couches, the women prepared
scented rubbing oils. Tsumoto, lying on his back, had
closed his eyes and now looked harmless enough—at least
for now. And if this was a trap, I had seen no indications
of any set up so far. For the moment, then, I was determined to enjoy myself.

When Lia bent over me a few minutes later, her hands
covered with scented oil, I saw that she had replaced her
dress with a towel that barely covered her breasts and
hips.

"Relax," she said. "And do not move." She whispered
the words as she pressed her hands gently over my face.
"Concentrate on feeling every muscle as I massage it. Let
your mind become one with your body."

I felt vulnerable to an attack by Tsumoto as I lay there,
so I took advantage of the silence to alter my consciousness and go into a light Yoga trance to heighten my hearing ability. Soon I was in a relaxed state of readiness and
could easily hear the murmur of Naomi's soothing voice
and Tsumoto's regular breathing.

Lia worked at my forehead with a series of lateral
strokes from the center of my face to the temple, using
her fingertips. Each move ended with a tiny circle over
the temple that made the entire side of my head tingle
with pleasure. She did similar strokes on my cheeks and
chin. Her touch was firm and professional.

After several minutes Lia removed the towel from my
midriff and began long strokes down my chest ending at
the groin. As she worked down onto my thighs, my mind

was working on two levels. I was in defensive contact with Tsumoto's breathing, waiting for the shift of rhythm that would signal a move, and in addition I was sorting out and integrating the conversation we had on the way here.

Tsumoto was obviously nothing more than a lower level flunky. I was certain of that from the way he talked and the things he had said. He was acting on someone else's orders, not being intelligent enough to be an independent agent. I figured he had been told Owen's background, but given the name Tsumoto to fit it into. He probably knew little beyond what he had told me about his so-called cousin. But I still had no idea what his purpose was here with me.

By the end of the hour all parts of my body had been thoroughly massaged and I was in a state of near euphoria. Lia topped off the treatment with an electric vibrator rubdown of almost every square inch of my skin. The gentle hum tickled each muscle back into readiness and energized deeper mental levels of consciousness.

I sat up and faced Tsumoto, noticing a momentary flicker of tension in his face. "Why was your cousin Tataka coming to the States?" I asked.

"Business," he said after a brief hesitation.

I fired several more quick questions at him, and he avoided answering each of them. He seemed to be lost in thought.

"Please come to the bath," Lia said, laying the vibrator on the low table between the shallow pool and the couches as she led the way.

Tsumoto and I were soon sitting in the clear, lukewarm water as the women prepared soaps and spice oil for the bath. When they were ready, they turned around, dropped their towels and moved slowly into the water with no rush to hide the smooth flesh of breasts and thigh and buttocks. They knelt in the bath and moved carefully behind us. I could feel Lia's firm breasts touch teasingly on my back as she stroked my shoulders and chest.

I relaxed once more. There was definitely an enjoyable sexual side to knowing that everything was being done for my pleasure and soon I would have Lia in bed. As if answering that thought, she snuggled closer and pressed her torso full against my back. Still kneeling, she brought her knees around my sides and nestled her soft groin against my lower back, her breasts against my upper back and shoulders. The scented water and oil made us slippery and smooth against each other.

I was drifting away again when I suddenly noticed a break in the rhythm of Tsumoto's breathing. Glancing toward him I could see his shoulder muscles tensing beneath Naomi's hands.

Just as I looked his way, he moved sharply and lunged toward the hand vibrator which was still plugged into the wall socket.

I immediately sprang toward him but he had anticipated my move and feinted to the right then swiveled back to the left, grabbed the vibrator and held it high above his head, turning toward us and emitting a high-pitched, "Banzai!" Then he plunged the vibrator toward the water.

I caught his wrist in both my hands and jerked upward, pulling the machine away just before it reached the surface. With both hands, Tsumoto gripped the electric death weapon and tried to force it downward again. I knew we would all be electrocuted if he succeeded. It took all my strength to prevent his second attempt, but I succeeded in pushing the vibrator high above our heads and holding it there for the moment.

Tsumoto glared silently at me, his face contorted in a maniacal rage. Suddenly he shifted his weight and kicked viciously at my knee. I jerked my leg back and avoided his attack, but my move gave him a slight advantage in balance and he brought the vibrator down to waist level.

We stood face to face, every muscle in our bodies straining to gain control of the situation, and, from that point on, ours was a strange fight. It was an intense minute of attacking and defending, all done in the silent graceful moves of Tai Chi, the slow-motion Kung Fu usually performed as a physical and spiritual exercise. I parried every attack he made, and he succeeded in blunting each of my attempts to gain control of the vibrator.

Finally Tsumoto let go with one hand and aimed a blow at my stomach which I burned away with my left hand. I saw my chance in that moment, twisting the vibrator upward and clockwise, wrenching it from his grip. But, before I could toss it to safety, he smashed the side of my neck with the side of his hand, held it high over his head and again screamed, "Banzai," then plunged it down toward the water.

I was too far off balance this time to stop him, and in the brief instant I had remaining, I managed somehow to flip backward up onto the carpeting. Only my heel was in the water when the sharp jolt of electric current shot through me, but it was only brief and harmless because I was completely out of the water a split second later.

As I lunged for the cord where it was plugged in halfway across the room, Naomi and Lia screamed and jerked spasmodically around the huge tub, while Tsumoto had fallen face first into the water and was grunting and thrashing like some huge wild pig gone suddenly berserk.

Within a few short seconds after the vibrator had hit the water I had the plug out, but it had been enough time to kill all three of them. A deathly silence descended over the room for a long moment as I stood, Wilhelmina in hand, looking down at the reddened bodies of the two women and the enigmatic Tsumoto.

Then someone screamed from another part of the building, and I could hear the sounds of footsteps pounding up the front stairs.

This was no time to stick around, I thought as I grabbed my clothes, then ducked out into the corridor and managed to make it through the back exit door before I was seen by anyone. When it came time to count bodies, they would wonder where the second man had gone, but I was certain the investigation would be brief and not very complete. Things like this were happening almost nightly in this unsavory section of the city.

In the alley behind the building, no one was around while I hurriedly dressed. Tsumoto was crazy, there was no doubt about that. His move had been clearly suicidal. But could he have also been some kind of a fanatic trying to kill me at the same time? It would not have surprised me if he had tried to kill me, because I was the lone American contact waiting for Owen Nashima at the airport when his plane had crashed. If Tsumoto's superiors were involved in the secret Owen had stumbled upon, then my presence at the airport waiting for Owen implicated me, too.

There was only one way to make headway in this situation now, I thought as I finished dressing and walked out into the street and mingled with the crowd. I first had to go to Washington and pursuade David Hawk that Owen's death was not the end, but merely the beginning of an important mission. Then I had to fly to Tokyo to see Owen Nashima's beautiful sister, Takeha, a woman I had met years before; a woman I had met and loved.

CHAPTER THREE

"Nick, I'm afraid the answer is no."

I stared at David Hawk and was momentarily at a loss for words because I had just entered his small, crowded Washington office without saying a word. As far as I knew, he had no idea what I was about to say, and yet he was already telling me no.

He indicated a chair, told me to sit down, and when I was settled he stared across the desk.

With his sleeves rolled up and his tie loosened at the neck, the operations chief of AXE, a man I had come to love and respect, looked at this moment very much the editor in chief of Amalgamated Press and Wire Services. His messy office even passed muster as a press office, but there was something in the glint, or was it twinkle, of his eye that made me slightly uneasy. Was he a mind reader too?

"You want to go to Tokyo to see Owen's sister, right?" Hawk said. "Well, the answer is no. I've got too many important things for you right now. Maybe later."

I smiled, relieved. "New information," I said tersely.

Hawk sat forward, a new look of interest on his face. After a moment he nodded for me to continue.

"I made contact with an agent passing himself as the cousin of Owen's cover."

"Go on," Hawk said softly. He lit his cigar, his eyes watching mine.

"He gave me a song and dance about knowing Owen's family," I said. "And then he tried to kill me. Ended up hurting himself in the process." I related the entire incident at the Oriental Fare, including my escape from any police inquiry.

"When did this happen?" he asked with a slight smile at my modest way of describing the action.

"Last night," I said. "Then I decided it was time to find out what Owen wanted to talk to me about. It must have been important, or else why the attempted hit?"

"And you want to go to Tokyo for that," Hawk added. He glanced past me at the green light over the door. The light signified that the room was safe. While it was lit, the electronic monitors AXE maintained were assuring us that no one or no piece of clandestine equipment was tuned into our conversation.

He rose and went to the lone window that overlooked Dupont Circle from the seventh floor. He scanned the skyline and studied the oval park for a long moment. I knew he was probably counting the young blacks who were pounding out a rhythm on congo drums near the fountain, wondering how many were possible cover men.

Finally, turning back to me, he said, "I first thought the crash was a coincidence that did not warrant your involvement. I need you for more pressing assignments."

"I felt that way too," I agreed. "Until . . ."

"Right," Hawk cut in. "Until someone appears out of nowhere with Nashima's cover name." He paused and waved a hand my way. "And then he tries to kill you." He smiled. "But you can take care of yourself. It's AXE's business that I'm concerned with."

"Someone was close enough to penetrate AXE's cover," I said.

"And that's bad for AXE any way you look at it," Hawk said. "I think you may be right about Tokyo. I'll put you out there as an Amalgamated special assignments reporter. Make up your own cover ident, and leave me a brief on it. We'll wire our Tokyo office to expect you." He stopped a moment and looked at me. "Just get in and get out as fast as you can without stirring up more than you have to. And don't vacation if nothing pans out on this. We need you here."

I nodded. "The FAA people sent the flight recorder

here as soon as they dug it out of the wreck. And they were more closed-mouthed about it than I've ever seen them before."

Hawk jotted a note. "I'll check into it," he said. "And Nick, no one but you and me knows why you'll be in Tokyo. Until you get instructions from me you're a free agent."

I had only partially heard his last words because a sudden memory of Owen had slipped into my conscious mind. Hawk must have recognized my somber expression, because he paused in mid-sentence and waited until I blinked and looked up again.

"He was a good man, Nick," Hawk said, his eyes unusually warm. "Good hunting out there," he said, and then he turned abruptly and went back to his paperwork.

I smiled sadly and stood up, checking my watch. "Time to catch my flight," I said when I was nearly to the door.

Hawk squinted suspiciously up at me from behind his typewriter. "You're already booked to Tokyo?" he growled.

I grinned.

He shook his head. "You're nearly as bad as I was at your age." He waved me out of his office. "Go on, get out of here, but don't forget the brief on your cover."

I flew to Los Angeles and changed planes to a 747, beginning the long trans-Pacific flight in late afternoon. The day was clear and bright, with only a trace of wispy clouds to mar the perfect purity of the upper atmosphere; the ocean smiled wide and blue below.

As usual the grandeur of the vast azure depths captivated me for the first hour, but then I became bored with the sameness of it and read a recent book on contemporary Japanese political history. By midnight I had finished the update on Japan and the plane was settling in for a landing in Hawaii. As we descended, the night lights of Maui and Molokai shown below like starry constellations outlining the coast. When we reached Honolulu, though, its lights were an entire Milky Way of stars, as if a wealthy giant treading the earth with a bag of diamonds had stumbled in the north Pacific and spilled his treasure over the southern coast of Oahu.

A lengthy holdover in Honolulu gave me the opportunity to call Tokyo to notify Taffy of my arrival. I gave no hint of my business, and only the cover name I had used years before told her my true identity.

We left Hawaii in early morning darkness and I slept most of the long night to Japan. It was mid-day when we arrived over Tokyo, the world's largest city, a vast flat expanse of houses and buildings, most of them built low to the ground because of the recurring earthquakes that made skyscrapers an impermanent enterprise.

During the trainride from the airport to the city's center, I became aware once again of the incredible density of Tokyo's ten million population. Even though it was not rush hour, the train was packed with workers and shoppers by the time it reached the station in the metropolitan area. From there I took a taxi downtown and saw the boulevards and side streets even more crowded than five years earlier. People were everywhere; an ever-present river of humanity.

But there was a more distinctly Western tone to the crowd now: we drove for blocks without seeing a kimono, while jeans and slacks and miniskirts were worn by all the young. The shops and signs and street vendors were eternally Japanese, however: a genuine and unchanging core of island Nipponese culture.

At last we arrived at my hotel, an old one called Tamako: Japanese for jewel. It was a cream stucco gargantua for Tokyo—sixteen stories high and an entire city block wide. I squeezed out of the cab and paid the driver, then turned to find my suitcase in the clutches of an intent bellhop waiting impatiently for me to follow. I let him carry it as far as the registration desk, then paid him two hundred yen and told him in Japanese to get lost. I didn't like the idea of having my weapons in someone else's hands.

After checking in, I traversed the vast white lobby, weaving my way through the greenery and sparse crowd. Delicate dwarf pine arranged near the chairs and couches gave the area the natural serenity of a sculptured garden. On the opposite side of the lobby was a bank of three old-fashioned elevators with strutted cage doors, and beside those were the telephones. Before going to my room on the sixteenth floor I phoned Taffy to say I had arrived, giving her my hotel. I had stayed at the Tamako before, so she knew where it was and said she would come right over. She had sounded excited to me, and I was looking forward to the prospect of seeing her once again.

As I hung up the telephone and went to the elevators, jet lag was settling into my head—that slight dullness of mind and slowness of reaction time due to too little sleep and too much external stimulation. The mind knows it should turn off and sleep, but the body keeps on churning to keep up with the pace of the surrounding world.

I pushed for the elevator and noticed the center one seemed to be out of order. Its door was open and the operator absent. Within a few seconds, though, a young man in a maroon uniform rushed past me and positioned himself at attention in front of the controls.

"Ready to go now," he said in my direction.

I stepped inside and turned to see several more people moving toward the entrance. The operator ignored them and pulled the inner doors shut with a rattling slam. The outer doors glided closed, and a twist of the circular control sent us upward.

The elevator was surprisingly large, with a capacity for twenty passengers, I estimated, and had evidently been installed with the original construction of the hotel. It had a low ceiling that fitted the shorter stature of the Japanese of a few decades ago. It is a fact that after World War II the caloric intake and consequent physical size of the

Japanese have increased. Children born after the war in Japan are taller and heavier than those born prior to the conflict.

We were almost to the sixteenth floor and I was thinking of how good it would be to see Taffy again, when the elevator came to a smooth halt. I picked up my bag and prepared to exit when I realized the operator had not opened the door. The row of lights above the door indicated we were between the fourteenth and fifteenth floors.

"What's going on?" I asked, looking closely at him for the first time.

He turned toward me, his face stern, and stood very straight as he pulled a narrow white shawl from his jacket and wrapped it around his neck.

"Death to my enemies," he said quietly in Japanese.

I quickly dropped my suitcase, expecting a lunge from him. Instead he whirled and lifted the emergency phone from its cradle and gave it a yank.

A terrific explosion went off directly above us with a dull compressive blast that left my ears ringing and my jet-lag head spinning.

The elevator swayed sickeningly for an instant, and then began to fall. My stomach heaved upward and I instinctively took a deep breath as we reached temporary freefall. But then the cables tightened and the elevator came to a lurching halt that sent both of us sprawling.

The operator recovered first, glancing upward with alarm. I followed his gaze as I got to my feet, listening to the low moan of steel cables stretching.

Suddenly I felt a loud snap at my neck and a burst of red filled my head as I was thrown violently against the side of the car, a searing pain exploding in my ear. As I fell, I realized that he had placed a perfect dropkick to the side of my head.

Almost senseless, I lay on the floor and tried to dodge his next attack. But I could barely think, much less move. My head was dizzy and bursting with pain as the maraud-

ing warrior over me leaped high into the air for another
kick at my head.

I dimly recognized he was aiming a death blow, but
there was no way for me to move fast enough to avoid it.

As he swooped downward, leg cocked and heel extended like the deadly talons of an attacking eagle, the elevator gave another lurch and dropped a few feet, bouncing
to a halt. At the same time, the lights flickered and
dimmed and the vicious kick fell short of my face by
inches. He stumbled awkwardly when his foot met nothing but thin air, and he fell over me.

All this happened in a split second, but it gave me just
enough time to recover and aim a blow at the major nerve
behind his thigh. I felt the solid thud as my fist rammed
home, then I rolled quickly to the opposite side of the car
and jumped up to see him limping. Taking a deep breath,
I shouted fiercely and spun in a tight circle, kicking out
with a karate slash to his chest.

But he slipped nimbly under the kick and lashed me
with a side-swipe to my right knee which hit home and
temporarily deadened my entire leg. I retreated to the far
wall, noticing that the escape hatch to the elevator car's
roof was slightly ajar, probably from when he had
crawled on top to pack explosives around the cable and
pulleys.

As the operator moved in low for another shot at my
disabled leg, I reached up and grabbed the ceiling hatch,
lifting myself off the floor and thrusting my left heel into
his face. I heard the bones of his nose crunch and disinte-
grate under the smashing blow, and I followed it with a
kick to the jaw. Again the satisfying sound of breaking
bone.

Dropping to the floor and crouching low, I slashed upward with a death-blow to his Adam's apple. I felt it
plunge home and knew the fight was over.

The operator stood motionless for a second after I hit
him for the last time, then grasped his neck in agony and
fell to his knees, blood flowing from his mouth and nose.

As he gasped and spat blood, the red also appeared in his eyes and he began to blink away the red tears. I knew his windpipe was crushed and blocked and that he would drown in his own blood within seconds. I watched as he wheezed and choked and finally fell forward, never taking his eyes off me. Gazing at the still body I did not have to check to know that he was dead.

The elevator began to slowly creep downward again, the cables humming with tension. Once the cables stretched beyond the rupture point, the molecular bonds in the steel would give way irreversibly and the cables would break.

I reached for the ceiling hatch once again and pulled myself up, pushing my head through. I saw immediately that the cables had been almost completely severed by the blast, and estimated that they would stretch a bit more, and not hold much longer.

Then I noticed a new danger. The pulley mechanism bolted to the roof, through which the cables ran, were severely damaged and were now connected to the elevator by the weakest of metal connections. It was nearly pitch-black on the roof, but the illumination from the open hatch beneath me enabled me to see that the bolts would not hold too much longer. They would break before the elevator could be moved to the next floor down.

A pulley bolt broke as I watched and the elevator went sharply down for a few inches, putting even more strain on the remaining bolts and tearing my grip off the hatch, sending me tumbling back into the elevator car.

I stared helplessly at the interior of what might become my coffin at any moment. There was no time to plan anything. Jumping up again, I pushed my suitcase up through the open hatch, deciding that route was my only chance for survival, even though it was a thin one at best. I pulled myself up through the hatch and out onto the roof of the elevator car.

It was darker on top than I thought it would be, so I moved cautiously to the side of the roof, reaching out to what looked like heavy vertical bars of some sort. They were the steel runners, I suddenly realized, that guided the car and kept it centered in the elevator shaft. There was no wall separating the three shafts for the adjacent elevators, only the bars at each corner. The runners were heavily greased, however, and there was no chance that I could use them to reach safety.

Another bolt broke with a shot, and now the pulley was at an odd angle, exerting even more strain on the remaining bolts.

I stepped quickly across to the front wall of the shaft, feeling frantically for a ledge or handhold, but everything I touched was smeared thickly with oil or grease. There was not a single thing to hang on to.

Another bolt snapped with a loud, sickening wrench and the pulley finally began to give way. I peered down at the depths of the shaft of the elevator to my left. Nothing but blackness.

Squinting down the one to my right, I saw only the black depths there too, at first, and I stood frozen with indecision, quickly calculating the chances of survival in a thirteen story fall if I were to lie flat on my back to distribute the impact over my entire torso. The chances did not seem high enough to tempt me.

Just as the pulley tore loose with a sickening jar, I saw a dim light in the shaft near me. I could not tell what it was or how far away it was, but it was moving up towards me, and I had no choice. I threw my suitcase down into the darkness and jumped.

For an agonizing moment or two I was falling through the blackness, and then I hit the roof of the adjacent elevator.

Scrambling quickly to my feet, I tore open the emergency hatch and dropped down into the car, smashing a glancing blow to the elevator operator's head with the back of my hand. He was down but not seriously injured. He might have a headache for a week or two but he would live. Meanwhile I did not want anyone asking questions of me, and counted my lucky stars there were no passengers in the car. As far as anyone in this hotel was concerned, I had been nowhere near that elevator in the next shaft.

As I started my elevator up to the sixteenth floor, there was a muted hum from the adjacent shaft, followed a few moments later by a splintering crash as the center elevator, the one I had been on, slammed to the bottom of its shaft one hundred and fifty feet below.

I stopped at the sixteenth floor and stepped out with my suitcase (which I had retrieved from the elevator roof) as if nothing had happened, although I felt as if I had been run over by a truck.

CHAPTER FOUR

An hour later three short raps sounded on the door of my room at the Tamako. I whipped Whilhelmina out of her holster and moved cautiously to position myself at one side of the sturdy wooden door, slipping the safety off the Luger and waiting in silence.

There were more knocks and then a feminine voice whispered, "Nick, it's Takeha."

It took a long moment for the voice to register on my still somewhat numbed brain, but when it did I relaxed and opened the door letting the woman glide past me into the room as I checked the corridor behind her. After the door was secure I turned back to Taffy who had been watching my every move. When she saw my bruised face and neck her eyes widened.

"My God, Nick, what happened?" she gasped.

I grinned a little too broadly and winced when the pain shot through my face and jaw where I had been kicked. "Does it look that bad?" I asked, soothing my jaw with my palm.

The expression on her face softened and she smiled slightly. "It can't be too serious if you can grin like that," she said, as she regarded me with mock gravity. "Badly swollen. Lopsided face. But no permanent damage. Maybe the work of an irate husband?" she laughed.

She stood silent then for a long moment, looking more beautiful and alluring than I'd remembered. Her hair was dark and straight and longer than before, framing her face which the years had transformed from youthful prettiness into the full beauty possessed by mature women. She stood, a study in soft fabric, wearing simple jeans and an unbleached cotton blouse embroidered with dark blue on the collar and shoulders.

I stepped forward and put an arm around her waist, pulling her close and bringing her lips to mine. I started to say how good it was to see her, but she closed her eyes and held her arms tightly around me and suddenly it was not time for talking. We kissed deeply and embraced for a long moment. It was almost like a visible relief for both of us after all these years, to finally be in each others arms. And now that we were together we did not have to rush it.

"God it's good to be with you," she said when we finally parted.

I kept my arms around her, savoring the feel of her firm breasts against my chest. She kissed my bruised face tenderly and then leaned back in my arms, frowning.

"Who did that?" she asked, concerned.

I released her without answering and went to the refrigerator set into a cluster of cabinets at one corner of the small room which passed as an efficiency apartment. "No one beat me up," I replied from across the room. "He got only one good blow in. It happened on the elevator."

"The elevator?" she said, her eyes even wider than before. "Nick, I saw. . . ." She let the sentence trail off.

I nodded as I clinked ice cubes into the glasses. "It fell shortly after I got out of it." I had to smile at her expression of fear. "Close call, but it's over now. Care for a drink?"

She nodded thoughtfully as she sat down on the aqua-green convertible sofa and curled her long legs beneath her. She became a dark haired blue feline adrift on a sea of green, and it did not surprise me that she drank her liquor neat. She had a wide assertive streak in her that I had always admired, though I had never learned exactly where it had come from.

"Tell me what happened," she said after we had made headway into our drinks. She seemed unusually interested in my condition for one accustomed to having an agent as a brother. Owen and I had never been talkative about our activities and I knew she had not been so curious the last time we had been together. It was just part of the code of living with or near people of our profession. One simply did not ask questions. Yet her wide almond eyes were pleading out of concern for me, I could see, so I gave in and related the elevator affair as I paced the room.

As she listened, the gentle lips, so soft when they smiled, hardened into a frown. "I was afraid of something like this," she said when I was finished.

For a moment, what she had said did not register on my brain as I gazed out the single window of the room at the night lights of Tokyo which seemed like billions of fireflies all hovering against a velvet backdrop, but then it hit home. How could she have expected the attack? And what exactly did she know about my mission or about Owen's work? I turned from the window.

"Did you expect trouble for me?" I asked.

"I knew Owen was on to something big," she said. Then as if she read the suspicion in my eyes, she slipped off her sandals and came to my side. "I'm an AXE cryptographer. I thought you knew," she said.

"You? A cryp?" I said, my surprise hardly concealed.

"Have been for the last two years," she replied.

"Must run in the family," I joked and regretted it immediately when I saw her hurt expression.

She shrugged. "Owen and I did not work together as you might have guessed," she said coolly and somewhat sharply. She sipped at her drink and her eyes told me that for at least tonight she did not want to talk about her troubled family.

Taffy and her brother were not close. They had never had a normal brother-sister relationship. She had been raised by her mother and her uncles in Tokyo while her father and Owen had traveled the world for business and adventure, reappearing at home at infrequent intervals. The uncles were surrogate fathers to her and held intense grudges against her real father because he moved from Tokyo to San Francisco six months before Japan attacked Pearl Harbor. It was an unforgivable sin to desert the fatherland, a sin the uncles never forgave.

And they pounded their bias into the daughter, transferring to that delicate vessel their spite and venom with a predictable outcome—the daughter grew to hate her father. Those same externally imposed resentments also blunted the natural affinity between siblings, preventing her from loving her brother in any way but the most formal.

When I had come to my first assignment in Japan, I had become involved with Taffy as well as Owen, and found myself to be a bridge between them. But that did not leave them any closer to each other once I had returned to the States.

"How did you know what he was working on?" I asked. "You didn't see much of each other, did you?"

"Not really," she said, moving back to the couch. "But I talked to him a week ago when he was in the office. He told me he was wrapping up a major case and had to go to the States to see you." She considered me for a moment. "Is that why you're here? Are you two working together again?"

"How much do you know about the mission he was on?" I asked, avoiding her question and postponing the bad news.

"He was unusually agitated about it," Taffy replied. "He spent a lot of time on it here and down in Hiroshima. But he never mentioned what exactly it was he was on to."

"How about the ciphers?" I asked. "Did he have you code anything for him?" I knew she might not want to give me that information, if there was any. It was an AXE dictum that employes did not discuss coded data with anyone. On the other hand, I was an AXE Killmaster and had access to the highest levels of classified information. I could demand any data I wished, and Taffy would have to comply.

But she shook her head. "He avoided messages altogether, except for the ones to Hawk arranging the San Francisco trip."

"No idea what he wanted to say to me?"

"The only hint I had was a slip he made last week when he mentioned a school of some sort in Hiroshima," she said thoughtfully. "He had been harried the last couple of weeks. And apprehensive too," she said, but then she suddenly looked up at me, her lips compressed to a fine line. "Nick, what did you mean when you asked me what Owen wanted to say to you? Haven't you seen him? Didn't he meet you in San Francisco?"

I hesitated, not knowing how to put the words.

"He must have met you there?" she said half rising from the couch. "Didn't he come back with you?"

"He never made it," I said quietly. "His flight crashed at San Francisco. I thought you might have heard."

She slumped back on the couch. "I've been sick the last couple of days. Haven't listened to the news or even looked at a newspaper." She looked up at me again, tears beginning to form at the corners of her eyes. "Nick. He's ... he's dead?"

I nodded.

The tears came then, and she fended them back for only a moment before she gave in completely. She let her empty glass fall to the floor and buried her face in her hands, sobbing deeply for a long while.

I sat calmly and finished my whiskey, letting her emotions run their full course. Finally her sobs diminished to sniffles, and her moans to deep sighs and she sat up.

She went into the bathroom without a word and after a few minutes returned, her composure restored. Her eyes were red and puffy, but she managed a weak smile.

"Sorry, Nick," she started, but I waved her off.

"He was your brother," I said. "I understand."

She nodded gratefully, and returned to the couch where

she sat down, her legs curled up beneath her. "Was it an accident?" she said.

I shook my head. "I don't think so, Taffy. Someone wanted Owen off their trail—permanently."

Taffy bit her lip. "And it almost cost you your life," she said in a barely audible voice. "I'd hate to lose you Nick. I don't think I could handle it."

It was not a happy evening from that moment, so for diversion I took Taffy out for dinner and a long walk through the Ginza—Tokyo's huge free-for-all Westernized district that boasted the largest and most modern department stores, shops and restaurants.

We did not say too much to each other for the remainder of the night, both of us nursing a mutual burden of sadness and regret for the occasions we had failed to spend with Owen while he was alive.

We strolled aimlessly, lost in thought, among the almost frantic shoppers and thrill-seeking tourists in the circus of the Ginza. And then we were back at my hotel room saying weary goodnights with lips and eyes too sad for lovemaking. I pulled out the sofabed and we both quickly fell asleep.

It was early morning when I felt her long, smooth leg thrown over mine, and her soft hands gently rubbing my back. Awakened by her touch, I came out of my slumber fully aroused, my eyes closed but my mind keenly focused on an intense kernal of sexual desire. Waves of warmth and tingling swept through my groin when she stroked the inside of my thigh.

"Nick," she whispered softly. "Are you awake?"

I turned over on my back and my hand brushed against the incredible softness of her breasts. I moaned involuntarily and pressed my lips deeply into hers, and held her so tightly that she gave a little animal-like squeal of pain and desire.

She turned on the lamp near the bed and looked at me with hunger in her eyes. "I want to see you . . . us . .," she said.

Then she was on top of me, pressing the full length of her body against mine, her breasts warm and full on my chest, her tongue wet and sensuous on my lips. My hands explored every inch of her satin smooth back and hips as we pulsed against each other.

I pushed her up and urgently sought her breasts with my tongue and she panted, straining against her desire, as I teased her nipples into a state of high excitement. Trembling, she clutched my hair with both of her hands and groaned with pleasure as she forced my head back onto the pillow.

Suddenly she was kneeling astride my stomach, her long hair falling over my face, her strong hands pinioning my wrists beside my head. In one smooth motion she raised and positioned herself, then came down softly to surround me with an incredibly warm and wet softness.

And then she swayed slowly from side to side and pulsed up and down as I arched upward to meet her every teasingly pleasurable motion. We floated as if asleep, adrift on an ocean of intense pleasure centered on the union of our two bodies; we lost ourselves and our sadness in a sexual sharing made poignantly sweet by the sorrow so close to the surface.

CHAPTER FIVE

As I entered the wire room on the fourth floor of Tokyo's Amalgamated Press and Wire Service, the harsh sound of typewriters being punished told me not much had changed in five years. With an affectionate arm around Taffy's trim waist, I ushered her in and waited at the familiar front counter separating the entrance from the madness beyond. A pert Japanese woman in a red pantsuit smiled as she swept from behind her desk and came our way.

"May I help you?" she said, pleasantly.

"I'm Nick Carstens," I said. "On assignment from the Washington office."

"We received word of your arrival yesterday," she said, lowering her eyes. The code name was my AXE identifier, which meant I was privy to the secret that Owen—the head man here—was dead, and she did not have to keep up the front. "Kazuka Akiyama. I'm the office manager," she said after a moment.

I nodded respectfully. She was in a difficult position at this time with her double life. On the one hand, she had to act the part of the office manager for the busy Amalgamated Press front operation while simultaneously being a professional intelligence agent and one of the top people in the AXE organization.

"I'll have to send a wire home to let them know I've arrived," I said.

"If you'll just follow me. . . ," she began, but I had to interrupt her, because she was indicating the way to the regular wire facility, which would not do for this message.

"Code gold," I said half under my breath.

Her eyes flickered only a trifle at the words, and she

continued her statement as if nothing out of the ordinary had happened. "Your wire can be composed immediately in one of our private offices, if you will just step this way, sir."

She led us through the maze of paper-cluttered desks, most of which were manned by Japanese or caucasian males who managed to look raggedly alike in spite of the obvious racial differences. Each had the rolled-up sleeves, the cigarette in the corner of the mouth and the slightly manic expression of all journalists under the gun for a deadline. The noise of more than a dozen chattering typewriters made my ears ring, but it was the perfect front for AXE operations.

It was the office manager's job to manage this anarchistic journalism enterprise and force it to behave reasonably; not an easy task when half the business passing across the counter was espionage and the other half legitimate press work. She knew identities and code names for hundreds of operatives who moved through the Tokyo office yearly, and had to juggle the two enterprises smoothly, for AXE missions were often handled at the counter while a crowd of unsuspecting Amalgamated Press customers innocently watched.

As we headed for a door in the back corner of the large newsroom, there was only an occasional glance at us from the writers and secretaries. They would have no reason to inspect us because Taffy was a regular there and only the softly spoken code words had identified me as a Killmaster, indicating I wanted my message sent top priority with the tightest security available. Yet the first hint the woman gave me that she had recognized the code was when she unlocked the rear door and showed us into a small room.

There was a hiss as the door settled into place with its airtight seal, and I found myself in a soundproofed room with walls smoothed over in B-46, a foam plastic which was a recent Army discovery. Anything from a whisper to a scream was absorbed by the material and converted into meaningless vibrations in the plastic bubbles of the walls. With the multi-laminate sintered carbon door, impregnable to anything below plastic explosives and small artillery, the room was perfect for secret communications.

I looked at the sparse furnishings and wondered what else was new in the office. There was a single desk and a few chairs with cabinets around the walls. A file cabinet and another metal cabinet aroused my suspicions when I noticed that they were attached to the cement floor with case hardened steel bolts, but my thoughts were interrupted when Kazuka secured the door.

"It's been a long time," she said. "We've added a few new things, this room included."

I glanced at her in surprise, studying her broad but not unpleasant face and alert eyes a moment before a glimmer of recognition flickered in my brain. "You were working here five years ago?" I said.

She nodded. "I began just before you and Owen started on that diamond smuggling problem the State Department wanted cleared up."

"Now I remember," I said.

"I was being trained then for the front office," she said.

"You've done a good job," I said.

She smiled, and once more became the professional. "The code gold?" she said.

"About Owen . . ." I started, but she cut me off.

"We know what happened, but not why. I presume that is why you are here, however."

I nodded.

"Then it is enough," she said with finality. "The code gold?" she asked again.

I sat at the desk and jotted the brief message to Hawk, describing the second attempt on my life and relating Taffy's comments about Hiroshima and the mysterious school Owen had mentioned but had refused to say more about. I also pushed Hawk about the flight recorder. After reading it and editing it, I sat back.

"Mind if I do the honors and send it?" Taffy said, reaching for the paper. It was the first thing she had said since we had arrived in the office.

I moved it out of her reach at the last moment, glancing up at Kazuka. "Is she code gold cleared?"

Kazuka nodded, and I turned back to Taffy. "Had to check it," I said, as I let her take the message.

She grinned and exited through a rear door which led to the top security coding room and secret wires.

Having a press service as a front for an espionage organization was a stroke of genius, I reflected as I watched the door swing shut with a hiss of air and lock with a heavy click. Virtually no one could tell that a few top secret wires were included among the hundreds coming into the building on a daily basis. And the piles of stories and newsprint in the offices made it unlikely anyone would search for significant messages among the scraps of paper.

Unlike other security and espionage services, we did not send our messages in obvious codes—not even in codes the enemy could not break, because just the fact that coded messages were leaving such a building as this would be the tip off that some clandestine organization was at work. Our codes were in the form of newspaper articles. Key words and datelines would alert the Washington AXE office that this particular story contained an AXE message. Cryptographers, like Taffy, would then process the story, gleaning the message and passing it on to the proper people.

"What else is new around here?" I asked conversationally after a moment.

A flare of indignation that I would make light talk at a time like this flashed across her face, but then faded into a warm smile. "Our operation hasn't changed too much since you and Owen worked together last," she said. "We've upgraded some of the equipment, but the footwork is the same."

"I noticed," I said dryly, looking around the small room.

She followed my gaze and smiled. "Owen spent a lot of time in here in the past year," she said.

I looked back at her and she seemed almost on the verge of tears. I was about to say something to comfort her, when she managed a smile.

"Do you still smoke those custom cigarettes? The ones with N.C. on the filter?" she said.

"How did you remember?" I asked incredulously.

"You left one in the office ashtray when you were here five years ago," she said smiling.

I reached into my pocket for the package, tapped one out and offered it to her. As I held my lighter for her and she took a deep drag, I found myself recoiling somewhat in disgust at that incident. "Not a good move for a Killmaster," I admitted ruefully.

"Not a good move for a Killmaster," Kazuka replied, "or for any operative." She tossed her head to the side and blew the smoke away from us. "I filed it in your AXE record."

"That's why Hawk is always all over my ass about those cigarettes," I said in momentary annoyance. But after a moment I had to smile. She was right, of course. "I always wondered what I had done that set him off that time. He never told me exactly, but he almost made me give up my cigarettes as a condition for promotion."

Kazuka laughed delightfully, and we bantered shop talk about ten more minutes, during which time I found myself becoming attracted to her. She was about to be propositioned when Taffy finally returned.

"Here's your original, Nick, and Hawk's reply already came in," she said, handing both of the messages to me. "That's an eyes-only copy for immediate destruction after reading," she added.

I nodded, and quickly scanned the operation chief's blunt and terse—as usual—message.

CARSTENS:
ARRIVING IN TWENTY-FOUR HOURS.
GO DEEP UNTIL MEET ARRANGED.
STOP ANY AND ALL OPERATIONS UNTIL
ARRIVAL.
OPS WASH.

I looked up, frowning. Instant concern was on
Kazuka's face.

"Trouble?" she said.

"I've got to go deep until the old man arrives," I said,
folding the pages.

"We can help with that. . . ," she started to say, but
Taffy interrupted her.

"I've got the perfect place," she said. "My uncle's
country house. It's about thirty miles from here in a secluded farming village."

I looked at the two women, my expression carefully
neutral. "Sounds good to me," I said to Taffy, then I
turned to Kazuka. "Secure enough for you?"

"It's your operation," she said nodding, but I was sure
I could detect a hint of disappointment in her expression.

"I'll stay there overnight, then," I said. "Be back here
tomorrow afternoon. I suppose he'll pick some out of the
ordinary haven for us."

Kazuka and Taffy laughed. They were both familiar
with Hawk's flair for clandestine meetings. The lengths to
which he'd sometimes go for security seemed ridiculous to
others in the organization. But then the operations chief
had never had his cover blown in his entire career, unlike
some of his critics.

Standing up to go, Kazuka took the papers from me
and slipped them into the slot of a gray metal cabinet near
the door. There was a click, then a muted hushing sound
as they fell through the opening.

"Laser incinerator," she said, unlocking the door to let
us out. "Absolutely no way to reconstruct the writing on
those pages, even if the by-products were collected. The

paper is annihilated down to the atomic level. Nothing is left but carbon dioxide and a few trace metals from the ink."

I smiled, thinking that the device was a far cry from the way movies handled such things. In the films I would have been required to eat the messages which would have been printed on rice paper. This was progress.

It was early evening by the time I had rented a car and we had escaped the smoggy dungeon of Tokyo's inner depths, but the sky was bright enough for us to see the free, open spaces of the mountains and meadows northwest of the city. We flew down the two lane blacktop in the large Honda, a new model with the biggest engine available. Since I had accepted Hawk's word and put aside more thought on the Nashima affair, we were in something of a holiday mood.

The countryside was spring green with the early rice crop emerging from the shallow terraced paddies that ringed the mountains. Elm and willow were sending forth shoots of palest green to challenge the brighter colors of bamboo and evergreen.

Ten miles out of Tokyo, the road was burrowed between walls of green, but open areas flying by gave us views of small villages nestled within the cleavage of shallow valleys. We had brief glimpses of thatched roofs and bamboo struts and dirt streets that marked the world of a few hundred gentle lives.

"Is your uncle's house in a village like this?" I asked about halfway there.

"It's near a small one named Kontoko," Taffy replied. "But it's rather secluded. Near a spring on the side of a mountain."

"Who is your uncle?" I said as I braked abruptly coming to a narrow bridge that crossed a mountain brook fed by spring rains.

"Yoshi Fujimoto," she said. "An elderly couple lives in his house and keeps it up for him. My uncle isn't there now."

Evening shadows covered the road as we entered a higher section of the mountains, where the road climbed and became more winding. It was at that point I realized we were being followed by a yellow Toyota maintaining its distance some twenty carlengths behind us. Soon the highway narrowed to a single lane, barely wide enough for two small cars to pass, and the Toyota sped up, following us at each turn.

"We've got a tail," I said finally, keeping an eye on them in the rearview mirror. I could just make out three heads in the car, silhouetted by the dim light from the full moon.

Taffy looked back. "Must have picked us up in the city," she said. "There is no way they could know where we are heading. We've got to lose them."

The road snaked deeper into the mountains and was virtually deserted except for us and the yellow Toyota.

"This road leads into Kontoko," she went on. "We'll have to get off it."

A bullet whined off the top of our car, and then a second bullet hit the pavement beside my door, spraying bits of tar and rock against the car. I jerked back in time to see a man lean out the window and raise his gun for a third shot, but at that moment the road curved sharply and he was thrown off balance as the car swerved.

I slammed the Honda into low gear and gave it all the power the engine could muster, whipping it around the mountain curves just below the critical speed at which the radial tires would lose traction and dump us down the steep incline to our left and into the yawning black abyss that would claim any car straying more than a few dangerous feet from the road.

The driver behind us must have learned his skills in a school for the weak of heart, because the Toyota began to fall behind, its lights lost to the curves and forests.

"Here, Nick!" Taffy shouted suddenly, as the head-lights of our Honda caught the light gray of a gravel road a few yards ahead.

I slammed the car into a lower gear, and with squealing tires we half slid off the pavement onto the extremely nar-row road that seemed to go straight up the side of the mountain through the trees. Cliffs rose to our right and dropped just as steeply to our left with only a few meager feet of gravel to separate driving vehicles from flying swallows.

Suddenly, darkness loomed ahead and I braked sharply to make the abrupt turn. The tires slid sickeningly and put us near enough to the edge to take our breaths away, then took hold and spun us safely around the curve.

After several similar turns, the road steadily climbing, I was dumbfounded to see the Toyota behind us, gaining ground. He had evidently seen the dust from the gravel road but I could not understand how he was not catching up with us unless he knew this road, which probably ended in some remote village—or on the mountaintop it-self. Either way we would be on foot and would have to face our assailants. I didn't like the odds.

After the next curve, I slammed on the brakes and slid to a halt, pulling the Honda into the pines as far to the side of the road as I could go. If there was to be a face-to-face confrontation, I wanted it to come with an element of surprise on my terms, not theirs.

I jumped out of the car and grabbed Wilhelmina, sta-tioning myself in the center of the road. I could hear the Toyota grinding gears, not too far down from us.

"I'll try to stop them with this." I shouted to Taffy as she climbed out of the car. "If it doesn't work, I'll try to draw them over the edge."

With a dull sound of rubber gripping tenuously to gravel, the yellow car burst around the curve a hundred yards down the road from us and roared directly at me. I knelt on the ground, held the Luger with both hands and squeezed off a shot. The right tire burst and the Toy-

ota swerved sharply to the right, but then pulled back on
the center of the road, its transmission whining under the
strain of the engine's power.

My second shot shattered a part of the windshield, but
the car kept coming. He was going to run us down no
matter what happened. If these people were anything like
the elevator operator had been, there would be little
chance I could stop them from this distance with only a
Luger.

I jumped up. "Don't move," I shouted to Taffy, who
was standing directly behind me, and I fired another shot
which smashed the car's left headlight.

At the last moment, with the car less than twenty yards
away, I started to jump toward the side of the road that
plunged down the steep cliff, but Taffy screamed my
name and grabbed my arm. There was no time to argue,
so I backhanded her across the mouth, and she went
down, releasing my arm, but grabbing tightly around my
legs. For a split second I was held immobile as the Toyota rushed down on us, but I kicked loose and dove
across the gravel and down the incline. My only hope, I
thought fleetingly as I went over the edge, was that there
would be a tree or something to grab hold of before I
went over the cliff itself.

Brush and small saplings tore at my face and hands,
and I was tumbling over and over, plowing down the hill-
side toward the cliff, until my flailing arms caught the
lower branches of a pine tree and I suddenly stopped.

At that same instant a rain of gravel and small rocks
spewed over the edge of the road, now twenty feet above
me, and like a rocket suddenly taking flight, the Toyota
came over the side, its one headlight curving to the right
in a lazy arc as the car overturned in mid-air and plunged
down the side of the mountain, its engine screaming
wildly out of control.

I could hear the car falling, the sound of its engine fad-
ing incredibly in the distance, and then there were the
sounds of metal smashing against rocks, and finally the

dull whump of the gasoline tank exploding. A bright orange glow shown through the trees from a spot hundreds of feet below me, and for several minutes I could do little more than sit hunched where I was against the last tree in my path before the steep hill ended in the shear drop of the cliff.

Carefully picking my way from tree to tree, avoiding the treacherous spots of loose debris, I made it back up to the road. Taffy was lying in the middle of the road, sobbing almost hysterically, and when I bent over and touched her to help her up, she snapped around and almost fainted.

"It's okay now, Taffy," I said.

"Nick. My God, I almost. . . ," she started to say, her eyes wide with fright.

"It's all right," I said again, helping her to her feet. And then she was in my arms, sobbing and crying my name over and over again.

I held her in my arms for what seemed like hours, until she finally calmed down. She looked into my eyes, hers red-rimmed and puffy.

"Nick darling," she stifled a sob. "My God, I almost killed you."

"Next time, listen to orders," I said softly, and not too sternly. She was genuinely sorry for what she had done, and yet there was something else in her expression, and in the incident itself that did not quite set right with me. People selected for AXE duty were usually chosen for their ability to remain calm under pressure. It was one of the prerequisites of the job. But then, she was only a cryptographer. Her duties rarely took her out of the office. She was not an operations type, and maybe I was being too hard on her.

Ten minutes later we were back in the Honda and working our way carefully back down the dirt road toward the highway, and Taffy was still crying softly.

"Don't worry about it," I said. "It's over, and it could have happened to anyone under fire."

She smiled weakly as we finally came to the highway and turned onto the blacktop. As we drove, the calmness and peace of the night air clearing my thinking, I hoped that her uncle's house would prove to be a more safe haven than my other accomodations had been recently. I had not had a decent night's rest since the air crash in San Francisco and I desperately needed to unwind.

CHAPTER SIX

The next morning I opened my eyes to more beauty than my half awake mind could bear, so I closed them and debated whether to focus on the kaleidoscope of bright garden flowers outside the bedroom or the smooth skin of Taffy Nashima who stood in tee-shirt and bikini panties gazing out the sliding doors. The warm tingle that spread through my body gave me the answer, but when I reopened my eyes, only the garden remained.

We had slept in the main room of the house on *futon* pads laid on the traditional *tatami* mats of rice straw which covered the floor. The walls were made of a thin, pressed fiberboard painted sky blue. Sliding doors covered with white paper led to the kitchen, the bathroom and the patio. As I surveyed the large rock garden from my vantage point on the sleeping pad, I was struck by the Spartan, yet beautiful appearance of the home. Only the garden showed the richness consistent with the wealth I knew Taffy's uncle possessed from his high-level position in the Fujimoto Steel Corporation. The house was simple to the point of being plain, except for a few pieces of sculpture within the main room.

Taffy appeared from the kitchen with a wooden spatula in her hand, and I became aware of the crackle and odor of something being fried Cantonese-style in a wok.

"Sleep okay last night?" she asked.

"Fine," I muttered, but watching her lean against the door, an enticing tilt to her head and a teasing smile on her face, I paid little attention to what she asked. She wore no bra and the tight shirt emphasized the fullness of her breasts. The muscles of her long thighs were toned and so well defined that they seemed to have been

59

sculpted by some master to flow perfectly from her hips to her delicate feet.

"Pepper and onion omelet sound good?" she inquired, smiling.

I threw aside the quilt and sat up, not letting my gaze deviate from the curves of her figure as I scanned her gorgeous body from her feet to the shiny black hair that framed her delicate face.

"Well?" she said in mock severity.

"Afterward," I said.

She grinned and disappeared back into the kitchen, soon followed by the sounds of pots and pans being moved, and then with a soft swish of bare feet brushing over tatami, she returned, completely nude.

"With or without the view of the garden?" she asked, hesitating near the open door.

"Leave them open," I said, and she glided across the room to me and lay down, her body stretched next to mine.

For the next hour we made love, the gentle mountain breezes caressing our bodies, and the sounds of birds and spring water running somewhere in the garden outside intruding on our conscious minds in the lulls. Japanese art is highly refined, and among the arts, lovemaking must have counted high on Taffy's list. I have made love to a number of women around the world, but very few of them could compare with her. What we had for that hour was not the frenzied, clutching lovemaking of frantic people, but rather the slow, loving and careful art of two people who were totally relaxed and confident of themselves.

The sun was much higher in the morning sky when I woke and found Taffy placing vegetables and eggs on a low table near me. She smiled and kissed me on the forehead when she saw I was awake.

"I didn't want to wake you, darling," she said softly. "You must have needed the rest."

I nodded and sat up on the *futon* for the second time

that morning, now recalling the several hours of sleep I had lost earlier that night when I went outside to scout the grounds, making sure no one had planned to surprise us during the night. It had turned cloudy and cold, and nothing had turned up during my complete exploration of the area. I had finally crept back inside to join Taffy under several layers of warm quilts.

As we ate, the previous night seemed a long time ago, almost in another century. I studied the flowers arranged among the rocky tiers wedged into the upslope of land to the left of the flagstone patio. There were reds and purples and yellows blended in harmonious swatches of color that showed the touch of a master. To the right of the patio were a pair of fruit trees whose swollen red buds looked ready to burst into pink blossoms of plum or cherry.

"Beautiful," I commented finally.

"The *papa-san* living here is an artist," she said. "And his wife is an expert in floral arrangements." She indicated a small vase of blossoms below a gold and red scroll.

"Your people take their art seriously," I said, not expecting a reply.

"It is the discipline," Taffy said, and I turned to her. She had a serious expression on her face.

"Like the Army?" I said.

She shook her head. "Nick, it is in everything we do. Our art, our government, our homes—even our family life. It's much more than what you Americans think of as discipline."

I had not intended for us to fall into such a deep, serious conversation, but she seemed to want it, almost need it. It was as if she were trying to explain something to me. Or maybe to herself.

"Are you disciplined?" I asked her.

She nodded solemnly. "Yes I am, Nick. All Japanese are. We have to be."

There was nothing for me to say to that, so I sipped

my tea and looked at her beautiful face for a long moment, before she finally broke into a wide grin.

"I'm sorry, Nick. It's just that I wanted you to understand," she said.

I returned her smile then looked at my watch, amazed to see it was barely nine o'clock.

"How about a bath, and then that walk to the village?" she suggested brightly, noticing my gesture.

I looked up. "A traditional bath?"

She nodded and sprung up. "Of course. This is a good Japanese house. The *ofuro* is in the bathroom. I'll get it ready. You just stay where you are."

A half hour later the bathwater had been brought to steaming by a small gas stove tucked out of sight in the metal enclosure beneath the gigantic tiled tub, and Taffy announced that it was ready. I rose from the cushion where I had been lying, looked once more out across the garden to the mountains beyond, and went into the bathroom which had its own set of doors opening to the patio.

Already nude and wet, Taffy pointed to a small pan of water and a soap dish for me, then stepped slowly into the deep tub submerging herself to the neck. I poured warm water over my shoulders and lathered up with soap, then scrubbed and rinsed off. After sliding open the doors to give us a view of the garden, I stepped gingerly into the water.

I expected it to be hot, but I had forgotten how blistering the Japanese preferred their bath water to be. Slowly I let myself sink into the scalding water, finally sitting all the way down with my back against the side of the tub, feeling the heat seep into my limbs, relaxing every muscle.

Garden fragrance wafted into the room with each cool breeze from the crisp morning that was slowly warming as the sun rose higher over the mountain and found a mirror of color among the flowers, firing them into brilliance and aroma with its light and heat.

I savored the smell with eyes closed, lulled by the heat

and the sounds of the wind through the trees. I could feel Taffy's presence near me, and when I finally opened my eyes she was studying my face, the serious look back on her face. Something was bothering her.

"What is it, Taffy?" I said quietly.

She seemed almost startled by the sound of my voice, and at first it seemed as if she did not want to talk, but then she shrugged. "I was thinking about Owen and my father."

"What about them?" I prodded gently.

"I want you to understand, Nick," she said. "It was different for us than for other Japanese families. Discipline is in my people's family life. We are taught obedience to the parents as children. Obey the elders; follow the orders of the Emperor."

"And your father left before the war," I prompted. She looked at me, an almost pleading expression in her eyes.

Taffy was choosing her words carefully now. "Confucius taught a way of living that is a social code which stresses *sensei*—obedience to the master. We still live by that code. It is honor."

"Until the honor was lost in the war," I said.

"The war changed a lot of things," she said. "The transition to new values is still not over. But new codes have begun to take hold here. Still, it does not excuse those who failed to live up to their *sensei*."

I did not know exactly what she was trying to tell me, but there was nothing I could say or do to help her, so I let her continue as I tried to bring to mind a mental picture of Owen the last time we had been together.

"I am living by my code, by the new *sensei* according to present days values. For me to step outside of that code is to dishonor myself. Just like it would have been a dishonor to me as well as my family, if I had stepped out of the old code."

"The Kamikaze pilot," I said.

"Exactly," Taffy said, her eyes gleaming. "Right or

wrong, they lived with their particular brand of *sensei*. It was honorable."

"Your father could not accept the old order," I said gently. "His values—his *sensei*—were with the West."

"Yes," she said, hanging her head.

"And he brought much dishonor to your family."

She nodded but said nothing.

"Finally, when Owen returned, you had to accept him because of the new order, the new codes, although your family could not forget the old *sensei*. You accepted him, but you could not love him as a brother."

"Yes . . . yes, God, yes, Nick," Taffy cried, looking up at me. "And yet. . . ." She stopped in mid-sentence.

"And yet you loved him despite it." I finished the sentence for her.

She nodded, and the tears began to stream down her cheeks.

We were silent for several long minutes until Taffy stopped crying, and seemed more in control of her emotions.

"I want to find his murderers," I said. "But I'll need your help."

She nodded and managed a slight smile. "You'll find them, Nick."

"What about those trips he took to Hiroshima?" I asked. "Did he say anything at all about what he was doing down there?"

"Only that it was important," she said.

"Taffy, I want you to concentrate on the last few times you and Owen were together. Try to remember what he was carrying, what he was reading or talking about. Something as simple as a single word in a casual conversation might be the clue we need."

She pursed her lips in thought for a moment, then shook her head. "Nothing out of the ordinary happened, Nick. The only thing I can remember about the last time I saw him was that he was carrying a large book about the war."

I thought about this for a long moment. "The only connection I can see between the war and Hiroshima is the atomic bombing of the city. But that's a long-dead issue now."

Taffy stared at me in silence for a long moment. When she spoke her voice was almost harsh. "The atomic bombing of Hiroshima is *not* a dead issue, Nick. It's a very real horror that still exists for those few survivors."

"I'm sorry, Taffy," I said, embarrassed.

We said nothing more to each other for the next ten minutes, until we finally climbed out of the bath, both of us pink from the heat. My skin felt numb, yet tingled when it was touched by the delicate breeze blowing in from the outside.

"I'm sorry, Nick," Taffy finally said when we were drying. "I didn't mean to spout off like that. It's just that I want to get this over with as fast as possible."

"We will," I said, taking her into my arms. "As soon as I meet with Hawk this afternoon, things will begin happening."

When we were dressed I packed our things in the Honda while she raided the kitchen for a light lunch of fruit and riceballs. We planned to visit the local village and walk through some of the surrounding countryside until it was time to leave for Tokyo. We would not be returning to the house.

A few minutes drive took us to a dirt road which led into Kontoko, a village of some forty dwellings, which we entered on foot after parking on the outskirts.

The road through the farming village was rutted and worn, and the houses had steep roofs of thatched straw, walls of weathered brown wood. Clusters of buildings were the rule instead of individual dwellings. The animal house, storage shed and the main dwelling were arranged around a central courtyard that contained fruit trees and perhaps flowers. The farmers smiled as we passed, seemingly giving us no more thought than if we were strolling the Ginza.

It was nearing noon and a stream of men from the fields moved lazily through the dust to their homes. They were dressed in black trousers and white shirts that seemed to be the traditional costume. Women were also coming in from the fields, their wide-brimmed, tan straw hats thrown back as they joked and laughed like groups of schoolgirls.

At the opposite side of the village, Taffy took me to the base of a steep path with crude log steps that disappeared up into the thick pine growth of the mountainside.

"We can eat near the shrine," she said as she led the way. "It's quiet."

We climbed for ten minutes, picking our way around boulders and over fallen trees, never straying too far from the spattering of gravel or the trodden grass that marked the trail. At last the incline leveled off into a knoll of cleared land ringed with bushes of red and purple blooms and covered with scraggly grass that grew poorly at that altitude and temperature. At the end of a courtyard behind a facade of fir and juniper was the shadowy bulk of the shrine, which from our vantage point looked like nothing more than a heavy roof supported by six round columns.

As we started toward the temple, the sounds of chanting reached us and we saw a group of monks standing to one side of the shrine. We moved to the opposite side of the knoll and sat down with our lunch out of sight of the holy men.

"This is a Shinto shrine," Taffy explained. "The Shinto are nature lovers, but above all they venerate one's ancestors."

"Is it a major religion in Japan?" I asked, the mission I would soon be deep into again that afternoon, and the danger it might bring along, seemed very remote in this magnificent setting.

"About half the population," she answered. "But it's

not really a religion as such, Nick. It has no dogma, no set beliefs. It's more of a spiritual attitude than a religion." She paused in thought for a moment, then continued. "Many Japanese are both Buddhists *and* Shintoists. When they pray for their ancestors, they are Shintoists. But when they meditate, they think of Buddha."

"I remember Owen saying something about his people being spiritual rather than dogmatic."

Taffy smiled wryly and shook her head. "Owen was an American."

"What's wrong with that?" I asked, only half teasing, but she took me seriously.

"Nothing for an American, but for a Japanese born. . . ." She let the sentence trail off when she saw the look of amusement in my eyes. She turned away. "We are spiritual . . . and idealistic too," she added.

I watched her as she gazed at the heights surrounding us, noticing how her hair fell over her ear and graced her shoulder. She was a deeply troubled girl; not the Taffy I remembered from five years earlier. Something had changed in her, and it had to do with her father and her brother. I only hoped that her confusion and troubled state of mind would not affect this mission. I was counting on her for help with Japanese customs and the language which I had not yet fully mastered.

"What did it do to your family when your father left for the States?" I asked softly, taking a stab in the dark.

She reacted almost too quickly, turning wary eyes on me. She did not speak for a long moment as she studied my face, and I could see an entire series of conflicting emotions cross her expression before her eyes finally softened. Once again she looked away, as if talking to me would be easier if she did not have to look at me.

"It tore us apart at first," she said in a far-away voice. "But then my uncle stepped in and took care of mother. He raised me as if I were his own daughter."

"And Owen?"

"He stayed with father, of course. But even after the war they spent little time with us."

I could see tears close to the surface of her emotions, so I changed the subject, and for awhile we talked about her job as an AXE cryp and about the States.

Ten minutes later the monks filed past in a slow, solemn procession, and disappeared down the path, leaving Taffy and me the only people on the mountain.

Later, exploring the temple, we found that the supporting columns and ceiling beams were carved out of solid mahogany logs, inlaid with mother of pearl and gold. The shrine itself was a relatively simple blue clay vase with delicate Greek-like curves and a wide mouth, placed atop a truncated stone pyramid. Our feet crunched loudly on the gravel in the solitary stillness as we circled to view the structure from all sides.

To me this shrine was like the Japanese people I would have to be dealing with in the next few days or weeks or however long this assignment took. The shrine was old like the people, its origins lost somewhere in history. It was delicately beautiful yet underlying that was a ruggedness—both apt descriptions of the people.

Running my fingers down one of the columns, I found the wood hard and smooth to the touch, but I could feel a carving in the wood that had escaped my attention. I stepped closer and looked carefully at the weathered column. A series of Japanese characters were carved along the column about five feet from the base. Among the few words I recognized was one—KAMIKAZE—and I shuddered involuntarily.

"What's the matter, Nick?" Taffy said, coming to my side.

I nodded at the carving, and she stepped closer to read it. After a moment she looked up and laughed. "Silly," she said. "It has nothing to do with the war. I thought you knew your Japanese history better than that."

"What does it mean?" I asked, completely at a loss as to what the joke was.

"*Kamikaze* means, literally, divine wind," she said, moving away from the gravel around the shrine to the grass. I moved along with her. "About seven hundred years ago a Mongol fleet with more than one hundred thousand soldiers set sail from China to invade our homeland. But a powerful typhoon swept in from the Pacific and entirely destroyed them. Without that, Japan would surely have fallen. Anyway, the storm was supposed to be sent by the gods to protect the fatherland. It was a 'divine wind'."

It was time now to head back to Tokyo and as Taffy and I carefully worked our way down the steep path into the village, and from there to our car, the stillness of the countryside made me somehow uneasy, or perhaps more aware of my anxiety of having so little direction in my investigation. I wanted to dig into the affair and come up with some hard facts pretty damn quick. And I hoped that Hawk felt the same way, because I was in no mood now to be put on another mission while Owen Nashima's death was switched to a back burner.

CHAPTER SEVEN

Hawk's message was waiting when we arrived at Amalgamated Press, but it still left me in the dark about exactly where the rendezvous was to be. I was directed to drive to the Yokosuka Naval Base, the gigantic and important U.S. military complex in the south part of Tokyo. Further information would be waiting for me there at the main gate.

I left the vicinity of Tokyo Station in the center of the city and headed south until I connected with the large Sotobori-Dori Avenue, which I followed west, checking constantly to see if anyone was tailing me. Although traffic was incredibly heavy, usual for Tokyo, no suspicious vehicles were on my trail, so I stayed on the freeway as it curved lazily northward and made a large circle around the Imperial Palace. I turned off in the vicinity of Korakuen Gardens and drove once more through the frantic traffic in the center of the city, circling back frequently to throw off any would-be followers I had missed on the first go-around.

Finally I was passing the Ginza and heading southwest on the Hibiya-Dori Avenue, and it was early afternoon by the time I breezed past the Tokyo Prince Hotel and the remarkable Tokyo Tower; an eastern Eiffel Tower whose thousand-foot-high pinnacle reared arrogantly above the city.

An hour later I saw the gray buildings and fences that surrounded Yokosuka, the sprawling deep-water port nestled in a natural harbor between Tokyo Bay and Sagami. Traffic around the base was thick, and it took another half hour for me to drive the final quarter mile to the main entrance.

Braking gently, I stopped the Honda at the gate, rolled down the window, and offered up my Amalgamated Press card to the somber young guard standing with his AR15 at ready position.

"Nick Carstens," I stated matter-of-factly. "Amalgamated Press."

He studied the card for a moment and stepped back into the guard station to consult a clipboard, then lifted a telephone and glanced back out at me as he spoke.

"Your escort will be here momentarily, Mr. Carstens," he said when he returned. "Your tour has been cleared through Base Command. You can park just inside the gate."

I thanked him and drove through the gate after it swung open, parking where he had indicated and lighting a cigarette for the wait. No more than a minute later, a dark blue station wagon raced diagonally across the lot and skidded to a halt beside me. The sailor who jumped out wore a duty white uniform with his cap cocked forward over short blond hair, and as he stepped toward my car he eyed me carefully as if deciding whether I was a person who would hold him to formalities.

"Nick Carstens?" he said as I got out of my car.

I nodded and extended my hand. "At ease, sailor. I'm a writer, not a general."

He relaxed noticably. "Ensign Wilburn," he said.

We got into his station wagon and sped toward the center of the base, turning onto a wide thoroughfare that roughly paralleled the shoreline. In the distance, antennae and towers atop ships in the dock area formed a jungle which rose over the tops of the buildings.

"You're going to tour the big baby?" Wilburn asked as we whipped past slower traffic, changing lanes frequently to avoid the congestion.

I nodded and smiled. "I'm sure you know more about it than I will after I see it," I said. I wanted him to talk about wherever I was going. I still had no idea where Hawk had set up the meeting. But apparently it was on some ship. I did not like Hawk's way of setting this up, but I did have to admit that security could hardly be broken if no one from AXE—myself included—knew exactly where the meeting was to take place. And those who did know where I was headed, did not know my real identity, nor did they know about the meeting. It was a neat set up. But cumbersome.

"Nope," Wilburn said after a moment. "Never been aboard a sub, much less a nuke."

"That makes two of us," I replied. "Where is it docked?"

"In the deepwater slips at the west end. We'll be there in just a couple more minutes." He concentrated on traffic, and when it finally seemed to thin out a little, he glanced my way again.

"What kind of stuff do you write?" he said conversationally.

Here it comes, I thought. The security net double-checking my story. I smiled inwardly at his obvious attempt. Quickly I reviewed what little I knew about the Navy, Naval Bases and ships in general. What I said to this young man would no doubt find its way to his superiors in intelligence, and although flunking his test would not place me in any jeopardy, it would make me look bad in Hawk's eyes. And that was something I did not want to happen.

"Routine stuff, mostly for Amalgamated," I said with only a very short pause. "But I've done some things for the service magazines. You know, *Military Affairs*, and *Navy Log*, things like that. But I've never done anything about a nuclear submarine. I'm looking forward to this today."

He flashed a smile. "What a life. Tour a sub and write a story, then move on to something new."

The harbor swept briskly by to our left as we sped down the loading wharfs toward the conning tower of a massive gray hulk whose smooth, low lines marked it as the nuclear submarine.

"You stationed here in Tokyo?" Wilburn asked.

"Stateside," I said.

"I suppose your bills go on an expense account?"

"Down to the last martini," I said, smiling.

"That's my style," Wilburn said, laughing. "How do I get into the business?"

"You serious?" I asked.

He nodded. "I'm in security now, but I think I'd like to get into something like you're doing."

I wondered for a moment if this was still another security game he was playing. He could not be that naïve, so I decided to play it safe. "When you have the time, check in with the station chief at Amalgamated Press here in Tokyo. Tell him who you are, what you'd like to do when you get out of the service, and he'll be able to help you. Tell him I gave you a recommendation." This way if he was really a budding newsman, the station chief would know where to send him. But if he wanted the secret service, the chief would also know how to handle it. Either way, I would not have to worry about it.

"Thanks," he said earnestly as we pulled up near another fence and gate. He nodded toward the guard house just inside the gate a few yards from the metal walkway which led down to the sub. "You're in their hands now. This is as far as I go."

"Thanks, sailor," I said, climbing out of the car. "Good luck, now."

After he was gone, I was escorted into the guard house by another young sailor. A phone call brought forth an escort who took me aboard and guided me through the labyrinth of corridors and stairwells leading into the bowels of the ship. The "Jefferson" was the latest addition to our fleet of missile-carrying subs, but as always, space aboard even the nukes was conserved to the last cubic centimeter, and ease of transit for sailors was not a prime consideration in its design. It was still a lot nicer than the last nuke I was on.

At last we stood in front of a polished wooden door

whose brass plate identified it as the Officers' Wardroom.
My guide rapped softly and stood at attention as a gray-
haired officer opened the door.

"Mr. Carstens, sir," the young man said.

"Thank you, Lieutenant. That will be all," the officer
said. Inside, he indicated a chair for me at a long table,
gave me a cup of coffee, then left without a word. I
sipped the hot coffee and listened to the distant clanks
and clanging of onboard activity as the sub was checked
out and refitted for its next voyage. After a few minutes,
Hawk barged unceremoniously into the wardroom, locked
the door behind him and turned toward me.

"Hello, Nick," he said gruffly. He studied the room for
several minutes, not moving from his position by the
door, until he seemed satisfied. He laid his briefcase on
the table and took out a cigar as he sat down across from
me. "Give me the latest," he said without preamble.

He filled the air of the confined room with his usual
unbearable smoke as I related the car chase and shootout
that had occurred on the way to the country hideaway,
and for completeness I described the elevator incident one
more time.

Hawk listened without interrupting as he smoked.
When I was finished, he thought a moment before he
spoke. "Have you looked through Owen's files in the office yet?"

"That was on my list of things to do," I said. "But your
stop order arrived before I had a chance. I figured it was
better for me to get out of the city immediately."

"Just so," Hawk said as he studied the half-finished
stogie in his hand. He opened his briefcase and took out
some papers. "No connection has turned up yet linking
Owen's work with the crash," he said. "But I do have a
connection between the crash that killed him and three
other similar incidents." He paused briefly, then continued. "What was the last major air disaster?" he said.

"The one in San Francisco, of course," I said. "Three
hundred and eleven people dead."

Hawk nodded. "And the one before that?"

"Three weeks ago in London. A Boeing 747. Close to three hundred dead in that one, too. It was in all the papers. . . ."

"You're right," Hawk said, cutting me off. "And the one before that?"

I searched my memory. "A DC-10 in Paris, I think. It wiped out half the terminal when it came down."

"More than four hundred killed in that one," Hawk added. "And two weeks prior to that another DC-10 went down on final approach at Kennedy and killed two hundred and ninety people." He pushed his chair away from the table, crossed his legs and began to speak softly, almost menacingly. From past experience I knew from his tone of voice that we were now getting down to the actual purpose of our meeting—a purpose that had brought Hawk halfway around the world to see me in person.

"What strikes you as being similar about all those crashes?" he asked softly.

"All were jumbo jets," I said hesitantly. I did not know what he was driving at. "High death tolls in all of them," I added.

"Exactly," he said dryly. "And every one of those planes was on final approach when they went out of control. Four major crashes in less than three months, with a total of more than thirteen hundred people dead." He stood up and paced the small space between the conference table and the wall. "I wouldn't have thought much of it if one of those silly FBI circulars they send around hadn't actually made some sense. They must have a few good brains somewhere in the Bureau, I guess, because someone noticed that the probability of those jets accidentally crashing within a few weeks of each other is extremely small. The big planes are engineered too well for that to happen by chance."

"So something's behind them all?" I asked.

"That's what I'm thinking," Hawk said. "I pushed the FBI a little, through channels, and they came up with transcripts of the flight recordings from the two U.S. crashes." He paused and raised an eyebrow. "They didn't want to cooperate, as usual, but when I finally read the transcripts I understood why. They were pretty damn strange." Hawk pushed the papers across the table toward me.

"The plane Owen was on...," he started, but then paused. "Hell, just read it yourself and draw your own conclusions."

I picked up the papers and saw from the title on the top sheet that it was an excerpt from the cockpit conversation aboard Northwest Orient Flight 721, recorded just minutes prior to the crash in which Owen was killed. A marginal notation, stated that relevant information about aircraft flight systems had been added parenthetically, and that translations from the Japanese had been performed by qualified National Security Agency linguists.

Leafing through the first few pages I learned that the aircraft had been given clearance to land and had begun its final approach with conversation between the pilot and co-pilot indicating no trouble with the plane. But at that point, the script indicated that a stewardess had knocked on the door and mumbled something unintelligible to those within:

Pilot: WHAT'S THAT?
Co-Pilot: SOUNDS LIKE JULIE. (Spoken more loudly): COME IN JULIE. (Sound of cabin door opening, then clicking shut.)
Pilot: WHAT THE HELL! YOU CAN'T BE IN HERE. WE'RE LANDING. GO BACK TO YOUR SEATS.
First man: (Translated from the Japanese): THE WINDS OF HEAVEN BLOW SWEETLY AGAIN.
Pilot: NO NEED TO USE THOSE GUNS OR WE'LL ALL GO DOWN TOGETHER.
(Brief pause)
Second man: (Spoken in English): WE'RE TAK-

ING CONTROL OF THIS AIRCRAFT. GET UP
FROM YOUR SEAT.

Co-pilot: NO! I HAVE TO BE HERE FOR THE
LANDING. REGULATIONS . . .

(Sounds of struggle)

Co-Pilot: BASTARDS!

(More struggle, followed by moaning . . . source unidentified.)

Pilot: TAKE IT EASY MAN, DAMN YOU!

(Unintelligible exchange in Japanese between the
two men)

(Sounds of movement.)

First man: WE WILL KILL WITHOUT HESITA-
TION IF YOUR RESISTANCE CONTINUES.

Pilot: DON'T HIT HIM AGAIN. I'LL COOPER-
ATE IF YOU'RE REASONABLE.

(Pause, then more sounds of movement within the
cabin)

Pilot: (Urgently) WHAT THE HELL ARE YOU
DOING? YOU CAN'T FLY THIS PLANE.

Second man: (Spoken to the first man in Japanese):
THE CONTROLS ARE FAMILIAR. I CAN
TAKE FULL COMMAND NOW.

Pilot: GET THE HELL OUT OF THAT SEAT.
WE'RE ON FINAL APPROACH AND I DON'T
WANT YOU NEAR THE CONTROLS, YOU
BASTARD.

(Sounds of a struggle)

Second man: (In Japanese): LEAVE HIM IN HIS
SEAT.

Control Tower: NORTHWEST SEVEN TWO
ONE. WE HAVE YOU ON FINAL FOR EIGHT.
ALTITUDE AND DESCENT LOOKING GOOD.
YOU NEED NOT ACKNOWLEDGE FURTHER
TRANS. . . . (the radio equipment is turned off at
this point.)

First man: THE TERMINAL.

Second man: AGREED. IT IS THE BEST WE CAN DO.

(Pause for several seconds.)

(Flight controls are adjusted at this point to put the aircraft into a left turn and a shallow dive. Full thrust is given to all engines. The aircraft is fully operational from this point to the time of impact.)

Second man: LIKE CHERRY BLOSSOMS IN THE SPRING, WE FALL CLEAN AND RADIANT.

(Loud noises of crash. Flight controls become disfunctional at this point) ADDENDUM: This point coincides with the aircraft collision against the control tower.

First man: DEATH IS LIGHTER THAN A FEATHER, BUT DUTY IS HIGHER THAN A MOUNTAIN.

(Loud crash sounds of a few seconds duration, after which flight recorder becomes disfunctional from an impact force of thirty-three G's.)

I scanned the entire transcript once more before I handed it back to Hawk, who immediately locked it in his briefcase. "Japanese terrorists?" I asked.

"Probably," Hawk said. "There also was a Japanese team involved in the other U.S. crash as well. There was a fight aboard that one. Not much of the recording makes much sense."

"How about the crashes in London and Paris?"

"No word yet. Might take days, even weeks, to get the flight recordings on those because those airlines were not American companies." He looked intently at me. "We're going out on a limb, Nick, but I'm convinced that Owen's work here had something to do with those crashes. That's why he was killed."

"Owen wouldn't have wasted much time if they were unconnected events. But there's a leak somewhere, and if that's true," I said, "they ... whoever they are ... knew he was onboard that flight."

"They're fanatics," Hawk said, chewing on his cigar. "But well organized and dedicated."

"I want to follow up what Owen was doing, sir," I said.

Hawk allowed a faint trace of a wry smile to play across his craggy features, and he nodded. "Right," he said. And then he got up. "A few minutes after I leave here, a Chief Petty Officer will pick you up, and give you a complete tour of this ship. That will keep your cover intact."

I said nothing, merely nodding.

He moved to the door, then stopped to face me once again. "One last thing, Nick," he said. "And it's important. I'm not completely convinced that AXE security was broken. The fact that someone knew Owen's cover ident doesn't prove it was inside information. Owen has used that cover before. And he probably used it as an Amalgamated Press reporter working on this story. If he stirred up enough trouble, they would have killed him thinking he was nothing more than a newsman."

"The AXE leak is unlikely," I said, agreeing with Hawk, but something inside of me was ringing a warning bell. This was too easy an explanation. It would just be one extra thing for me to check.

"If it *was* an AXE leak, however," Hawk said ominously. "You know what was be done."

"Unconditional termination," I said. "Yes, sir."

"Absolutely," he snapped. "And since you are on foreign soil, and there might be trouble prosecuting a national, it is doubly imperative that such an individual not survive the span of your assignment." With that, Hawk opened the door and disappeared down the ship's narrow corridor, leaving only the cold echo of footsteps on metal to underscore his words.

CHAPTER EIGHT

It was nearly six o'clock by the time I was finished with the tour of the Jefferson and once again in the hands of Ensign Wilburn who was my escort to the main gate. I suppose I should have been impressed by what I had seen, but Hawk's comments and the script from the flight recorder aboard Owen's flight hung like a heavy fog in my mind.

"Must have been some ship," Wilburn was saying, and I looked up at him.

"Sorry. Guess I was daydreaming," I said.

"Quite a ship, I was saying," Wilburn repeated as he sped along the main thoroughfare toward the gate.

I nodded. "It'll make a great story."

We drove for the next few minutes in silence, my mind racing to a dozen different possible angles of attack on this case—rejecting each for one reason or another—until we pulled up at the main gate near my car. Wilburn turned to me.

"You doing anything tonight?" he said. "I thought maybe we could find a couple of chicks and . . ."

I cut him off. "Think I'll take a rain check, Ensign. I've got a lot of work to do. Have to get this story out in the next few days. Can't keep my boss waiting, you know."

"Right," Wilburn said, obviously disappointed. "Anyway, it was nice meeting you. And good luck."

"Thanks," I mumbled and got out of his car and into my own.

The guard waved me on, and soon I was heading back toward the center of Tokyo, my mind only half on the traffic which was extremely dense from late shift workers on their way to the many factories surrounding the city.

That there was some connection between all the air disasters that had occurred recently, or at least the two in the States, was a foregone conclusion from the flight recorder transcripts Hawk had shown me. And I would have bet my last dollar that the flight recordings from the other two crashes would come up with similar situations. But the connection between what Owen was working on and those crashes was considerably more thin.

I pulled onto the main expressway which led directly into the center of the city, merged smoothly with the rapidly flowing traffic, and tried to tick off the relevant points in my mind.

First: Owen was working on something that was so important he could not trust it to routine AXE communications channels. That case had something to do with Hiroshima and possibly the war, if Taffy was correct when she told me she had seen Owen carrying around a history book before he left.

But I would need more information about exactly what Owen had been doing the last few days or weeks before he called me. Kazuka, the office manager, would help me go through his files for that information.

Second: In all probability, Owen had assumed the cover identity of Tataka Tsumoto during much of his investigation here in Tokyo and down in Hiroshima. That meant that anyone opposed to what he was doing could have known his name. But why transmit that name to an agent in San Francisco? And what did they want with his personal effects once he was dead? But more importantly, how did they know Owen's real background—aside from his connection with AXE itself—unless Owen had used some of his personal life as convincing background for his cover ident? But that seemed too complicated, too far out in left field.

But that, at least, I thought as I swerved to avoid a large truck that had swung into my path, was one connection between Owen's death and what he was working on. It was not a particularly good or solid connection, but it was a beginning. And it was good enough for me.

So, assuming Owen's plane was crashed to get rid of him, and assuming his plane crash was related to the others, what did they all have in common? For that question I had no real answer, not even a glimmering of an answer, but I suspected that when I did find the connection I would be very close to finding out what it was Owen had been working on.

Third: I ticked off the next point in my mind. My admitting that I was a close personal friend of Tsumoto linked me with Owen and his investigations. Therefore, the attempt on my life in San Francisco by the man claiming to be Owen's cousin. And that incident bothered me the more I thought about it. The man was apparently ready and willing to die just to kill me.

I almost jammed on my brakes in the middle of the busy highway when the connection hit home, and several drivers honked their horns angrily at me.

Of course there was a connection! The Japanese men in the airplanes had been willing to die for their act of terrorism. The man who claimed to be Owen's cousin was ready to die to kill me, as was the elevator operator here in Tokyo and apparently as were the men in the car that had followed us to Taffy's hideaway.

But once again I was brought up short. What the hell kind of people was I dealing with, who were willing to die so easily? Or had all those incidents been coincidences? Had the man in the Chinese baths been planning to jump out of the tub at the last moment? Had the elevator operator an escape route planned? And did the men in the car really mean to kill themselves in the attempt on my life?

There were only three things I could do for the moment. And unless something turned up with one of those things, I would be stuck. First were the men who had tried to kill me. The man in San Francisco was inaccessible as were the men from the car. But the elevator operator. His body was most likely at the city morgue, along with his belongings.

A half-mile later, near the last exit into the city proper, I pulled off the highway to a service station. At a phone booth there I looked up the address for the city morgue, which turned out to be not too far from the Amalgamated Press offices.

Getting back into my car, I merged with traffic once again on the highway and sped into the heart of Tokyo. If nothing turned up at the morgue, I still had Owen's files to look through, and then some snooping to do around Hiroshima. Something was bound to turn up, I was sure of it.

It was after seven o'clock when I finally found a parking spot half a block from the Tokyo City Morgue in the City Government Complex. I had made a date to pick Taffy up at her apartment at eight o'clock and take her out to dinner, but I figured it would not take very long here. Either I would be allowed to see the elevator operator's body and his belongings—which would only take a few minutes—or I would be thrown out on my ear. In which case I'd be back later. Either way, I figured I'd make my date.

Just inside the building, I stopped at the information desk which at this hour was manned by a sleepy old man in a guard's uniform. He directed me down one floor to the morgue, but said normal visiting hours were over.

"I'm with Amalgamated Press," I said to him in Japanese, showing him my card. "On an assignment. I'm doing a story about that elevator crash at the Tamako Hotel. You remember it from the other day?"

The guard nodded sleepily. "Yessir, but I do not think they will help you downstairs. They are all ghouls, and have no souls."

I smiled and nodded. "I'll try anyway. Thanks."

He nodded again, and pointed the way to the stairs. The elevators, he told me, were not in operation at this hour.

Down the one flight of stairs, and through a white

metal door at the bottom, I found myself in a very tiny, spotlessly white room that was completely devoid of any furnishings. The only things that marred the clean white surfaces of the walls, ceiling and floor were the door I had come through, another similar door on the opposite side of the room, a light fixture in the ceiling and a grille with a button next to it on the wall. The Japanese inscription beneath the button was the equivalent of the American "Ring for Service."

I crossed the room, pushed the button and a moment later a man's voice blared from the speaker in Japanese. "Yes? Who is it please?"

"Nick Carstens," I said in Japanese. "I'm with Amalgamated Press. I would like some information about a man you have here."

"I am sorry. You will have to return in the morning. No information this evening."

"But I'm on a story," I protested. "I have a deadline. I want to see the elevator operator who died at the Tamako Hotel the day before yesterday."

"I am sorry sir, that is not possible," the voice from the grilled blared. The man, whoever and wherever he was, sounded impatient. "The relatives have claimed the body."

"Have they picked it up yet?" I asked in desperation.

"No sir," the voice said. "They will come for it in the morning. Perhaps if you return early. . . ."

"Thank you," I said and stalked out of the room. I was going to return early all right. But much earlier than he expected.

Back upstairs, I learned from the guard that attendants would be on duty downstairs only until midnight. After that time, any bodies that needed to be brought to the morgue would have to be taken to a hospital until seven in the morning when they could be transferred here. It was a perfect set-up for me.

Taffy's apartment was in the fashionable Gensing-Ki District of Tokyo, and I had no difficulty in finding it with the directions she had given me earlier in the day. I did, however, take the precaution of parking my rented car two blocks away and traveling the remaining distance on foot, going twice around the block checking for the existance of any possible tails before I entered the three-story apartment building.

Despite my highly Westernized tastes—or, more accurately, European tastes—I have always had a fondness for the Oriental style in decorations and architecture. Taffy's apartment was no disappointment, and in fact was almost as pleasant a retreat as was her uncle's beautiful house in which we had stayed in the mountains.

I had been correct in my earlier estimation of her personality and the color that would best suit it: aquamarine, which made her seem like a soft, sleek feline animal, and the color was used to the best example in her small, three-room apartment. Alternating floor tiles, paintings and some floral arrangements, as well as the furniture, were done in various shades of that color, and it seemed as if she was afloat in the gentle South Pacific. With her and this apartment and several hours to kill, it was going to be an irresistable combination.

Taffy let me into her apartment without a word, and she stood staring at me, open-mouthed, trying to form words, but nothing was coming out.

"What's the matter," I said, instantly concerned about her. "Has someone been here?"

"No ... no ... oh, Nick darling, I thought something had happened to you," she managed to stammer. "I called the office and they said you had finished with the tour almost two hours ago. I thought you had been ... been...." The words were choked off and suddenly she was in my arms, the gentle perfume from her neck wafting up in my nose.

We stood like that for several moments until she began to calm down.

"I may have found something. At least a start of something anyway," I said.

She studied my eyes for a long moment, a curious expression on her face. "What did you find, Nick?"

"At the City Morgue. The elevator operator's body is still there," I said. "I'm going back tonight to have a look at it and his personal belongings."

"They're not open tonight," she blurted.

I smiled. "I know. They close at midnight."

"But can't you do it tomorrow? Through channels? Use your cover identity. Is it worth the risk of breaking in there tonight?" She sounded frightened.

"Take it easy," I said as lightly as possible. "Nothing is going to happen. I just want to take a look around, that's all. And it has to be tonight. The relatives are coming up in the morning to claim the body."

She started to protest again, but I took her into my arms and kissed her. She stiffened up at first, but then relaxed and soon we were in bed together, and although I thought that nothing could ever match the lovemaking we had at her uncle's mountain house, this evening's session topped the earlier match. Taffy was superb, and for a time it seemed like there was nothing of any importance anywhere in the world except for right here and now. Nothing mattered; not Hawk, not Owen's death, not my assignment—nothing.

I must have been tired, because the next thing I remember was waking up sprawled flat on my back across Taffy's bed. When I opened my eyes she was looking down at me from where she sat on the edge of the bed.

"Good morning, sleepyhead," she purred softly, and leaned down to kiss me, her soft, delicate breasts brushing my chest.

For a moment her comment did not register, but then I pushed her aside and snapped completely awake. "Morning?"

"Figure of speech, darling," she said, getting up laughing. "Actually it's just a little after one. If you hadn't

awakened, I was going to get you up. But I didn't want to
disturb you until now. You were out like a light. Looked
as if you needed the sleep."

I looked up at her and smiled. "Thanks," I said. "I
guess I must have."

By the time I had showered and dressed, Taffy had the
coffee ready for me, and unlike her earlier attitude she
now seemed resigned to the fact that I was determined to
check out the elevator operator's body at the morgue, and
she offered no further argument. When I left her apartment we kissed deeply, and she promised to wait up for
me.

It was nearly two o'clock by the time I had made it on
foot to where I had parked my car, and a quick examination of the door locks, which I had smeared with dust
from the road, showed that the car had not been disturbed
in my absence.

Taffy's perfume still lingered in my mind as I got into
the car, started it and headed downtown to the morgue.
What I would find there remained to be seen, and I don't
even know if I really expected to find anything of significance. But it was a loose end in this case, and I have
come to despise loose ends of any kind.

I parked my car two blocks away from the City Government complex of buildings which housed, among other
things, the city police force as well as the morgue. The
last thing I wanted to happen now was to be picked up by
the local police. Although a quick call to Washington
would verify who I was, I had a gut feeling that this case
was a big one, and it was a very real possibility that there
were informers within the local law enforcement agency.
No, I did not want to risk a blown cover. Not just yet.

Several people were still up and about which was not
unusual for a city of this size. It has been said that Tokyo
never sleeps—the same I suppose could be said of New
York, Paris, Copenhagen, or any large city of any con-

tinent. But tonight that fact could prove to be troublesome if I did not watch my step.

Ten minutes later I made it to the entrance of the city morgue and as I expected the lights had been turned off, the door locked and the guard who had been positioned just inside the door was nowhere to be seen.

The building was a large one of gray stone that stretched each way from the entrance for at least a half a block, and I was sure it was at least a half block deep. It was like most other government buildings the world 'round, I suppose, with a parking area of some sort at the rear, and some kind of an entrance ramp for the morgue itself.

I walked hurriedly to the far end of the building, where a driveway cut between the next building in the government complex. Making sure no one was passing by, I ducked down the dimly lit alleyway which led for about seventy-five yards behind the building, where it branched off to the left toward an open parking area, and to the right down a dark ramp beneath the building. This was probably the ambulance entrance for the morgue.

Moving down the ramp, I came up short against a metal garage door that was tightly locked. But set to one side was the service entrance, with another button and a "Ring for Service" sign. Shining my light on the lock set flush into the door, I had to smile. Everything back in the states, it seemed, had the tag "Made In Japan" stamped on it, while this lock on this door in Tokyo was a good old American Yale. Simple.

Taking a thin needle out of the lining in the lapel of my coat, I had the lock picked in a few seconds, the combinations of tumblers and slides easier to operate than many locks I have worked on. And only the most complete examination with the lock apart would reveal that it had been picked and not opened this night with a key.

A few moments later I was inside, the door closed behind me, and I held my breath listening for sounds, any sounds to indicate that I was not alone.

I was in a small room equipped with three stainless steel tables on wheels that evidently were used to transport corpses into the morgue itself. A pair of swinging doors were set into the opposite wall from where I stood, and I moved to them now making absolutely no noise.

I carefully pushed open one of the doors and peered through the narrow opening in time to see a flash of light, dim, and across what appeared to be quite a large room. I held my breath again waiting for any noise, and strained to catch another glimpse of the light. And then I heard it.

One man ... no, two of them were across the room. I could see them now that my eyes were adjusting to the almost total darkness. It looked as if they were bent over something. It looked like a drawer, and then I realized that this was the central storage area for corpses. The two men, whoever they were, evidently were looking at one of the bodies, and it was a good bet that the body they were examining was the dead elevator operator's from the hotel.

I could hear the two men talking, but they were speaking too low for me to make out what they were saying over the hum of the air conditioners.

Estimating the distance from me to them at about thirty feet, I carefully reached inside my trousers and plucked Pierre, my tiny but highly effective and silent gas bomb, from its pouch, pulled the pin and threw it in their direction.

At the same moment Pierre hit the floor behind the two men, I ducked back into the anteroom, flattened myself against the outside door, and began my countdown.

When I had reached a full sixty seconds, I cautiously made my way back to the swinging doors and peeked inside. Both men lay crumpled near the opened body drawer and, as I expected, the air conditioners had taken care of the gas so that the room was now safe for me to enter.

There would be a lingering smell of something undefinable for a few minutes more, but by the time this place opened for business again in the morning, the gas would be virtually undetectible.

Moving quickly across the room to the men, I checked to make sure they were dead. Neither of them had any identification on them, but both were armed and both were carrying in their jacket pockets the same kind of white shawl that the elevator operator had put around his neck moments before he had set the bomb off.

The shawls obviously were some kind of a connection, although at this moment what they meant was beyond me. I put both of them in my pocket, picked up the flashlight one of them had dropped and looked into the body box. The mangled body of a man lay stretched out inside, the sheet over him thrown back. Although his face had been somewhat mutilated by the crash of the elevator I easily recognized the elevator operator.

It was a connection. Obviously these two men were not his relatives, if indeed any relatives were actually coming up tomorrow to claim him. But these two, like me, had broken into the morgue to see him. But why? What had they been looking for? What was so important to them that they would risk breaking in here with the city police headquarters just a hundred yards away?

I pulled the refrigerated body box all the way out on its runners, threw back the sheet and quickly searched the compartment. At first I found nothing except for a plain manila envelope that contained only the man's false teeth, a watch and a ring. Another large envelope contained his clothing. But then the corner of something white and fringed tucked in under the man's legs caught in the beam of the flashlight.

I lifted the corpse's stiff, cold legs, and pulled out the bloodied shawl he had used in the elevator. It was exactly the same kind of shawl the two men I had just killed were carrying. This is what they had been looking for. It had to be. It was the only thing here that seemed to have any significance.

Tucking the elevator operator's shawl into my pocket

with the others, I flipped the sheet back over his body and pushed the drawer closed, then I pulled open several other drawers set into the long wall until I found two empty ones.

No one could know that there had been intruders here this evening, except for whoever had sent these men. If there were others directing these two, and I suspected there were, their disappearance might bring them out of the woodwork after me, which was exactly what I wanted.

I quickly undressed the two men, then heaved their bodies into the drawers. I stuffed their clothing and other personal belongings in manilla envelopes, flipped the sheets over each of their bodies and closed the drawers. And then it suddenly hit me what I had done.

I had become so jumpy and ultra-tense over the past days that I had simply killed these two, no questions asked. What if they had been mere intruders with no connection to this case? What would that have made me?

I have never felt good about killing anyone, even in the line of duty, but tonight I was having recriminations. This time I had been lucky. These men, as it turned out, were part of whatever was going on with this case, and would not have hesitated a moment to kill me. But the next time ... I let that thought trail off in my mind, for a moment. The next time I would have to be more careful.

It would take days for anyone at the morgue to discover the two extra bodies and wonder where they had come from. And it might take weeks until the bodies were identified and the lock on the back door finally checked. And even then they would have no idea who could have done this. By that time, I would be long finished with this assignment and probably deep into another one.

Checking the elevator operator's drawer front for a name, I was disappointed to find only a number, which evidently corresponded to some file in another part of this building. There would be no time for that tonight.

Stepping back away from the wall, I surveyed the entire room with the flashlight I had picked up. Everything seemed in order and there would be nothing for the authorities to find. Then my flashlight glinted on something metal. I stepped forward and picked up the object which turned out to be the metal casing for my spent gas bomb. I stuffed it into my pocket, cursing my muddle-headedness this evening, and then hurried out of the room.

At the outside door, I stopped and listened to make sure no one was moving outside and then I opened the door and stepped out into the muzzle of a waiting gun held by the largest Japanese man I had ever seen in my life.

"Are they dead?" the man asked me urgently, but softly in Japanese.

"No," I said, my mind reeling. Who the hell was this character, and how did he know I was inside?

He cocked the hammer back on the .38. "You lie."

I backed up a little, my shoulders pressed tightly against the door frame. "They're dead," I admitted.

"The bodies, where are they?" he hissed.

"In lockers. No one will find them for a while."

"My compliments on a job well done, Mr. Carstens," the man said, still in Japanese, and the expression on my face must have told him I was stunned. He smiled. "We know many things about you Mr. Carstens . . . or should I say Mr. Nick Carter, of late from San Francisco in California." The man hesitated just a moment, backed up a couple of feet and waved the gun for me to move forward out of the doorway.

"Lock the door, Mr. Carter, and come with me," he said.

There was nothing for me to do but comply; he was holding all the aces. I stepped forward, locked the door behind me, and then headed up the ramp with him a couple of feet behind me.

If we got all the way out to the street in front, there would be little or nothing I could do without attracting too much attention, and I did not want that. So my move had to come now.

I feinted a stumble, going half down on my knees, which brought the man up close to me. At the same instant that he was trying to maintain his balance and not fall over me, I punched up hard and viciously into his groin and he was down with a grunt and rush of air from his lungs. In the next instant I had Hugo, my needle-thin stiletto, in hand and was on top of him, the slender blade just touching the man's throbbing carotid artery.

"Who sent you?" I said in Japanese, but the man's eyes were bulging out of their sockets, and the saliva was running down the sides of his mouth.

"Quickly," I said quietly, but with force. "I will kill you now. Who sent you?"

Suddenly a light seemed to shine in the man's eyes, and he smiled, then shouted "Banzai, Aki Shintu," as he lunged upward sending Hugo deep into his throat. At the last instant of his life, he managed to twist sharply to the right, causing the blade to slit open half his neck.

I reared back, pulling the stiletto out of his throat, but it was too late. He was already beyond help, and even as I watched, the blood slowed and then finally stopped pumping from his torn throat as his heart stopped.

It took me several long minutes before I could think to pull out a handkerchief and wipe the blood off my hands and Hugo, then examine the man's pockets. Like the others, he carried no identification, but also like the others he carried one of the white shawls in his pocket. That made four of them I had found so far.

For a few brief moments I debated whether or not I should try to hide the body, but then decided against it. It would be useless because the concrete in the driveway was stained with his blood. Even when they found him in the morning, though, there would be no connection with me. At least not by the authorities. It was sloppy, but it could not be helped. For now, I had a puzzle on my hands. The shawls. What the hell could they mean? And what or who was Aki Shihtu?

CHAPTER NINE

I sat in my car for several minutes, the engine idling, as I calmed down from what had just happened. I could almost feel the adrenalin recede back to wherever it came from to make ready for the next time it was needed. What I had to have now were some answers, and fast. The deeper I got into this case, the more confusing everything seemed to become.

I had not really expected to meet anyone at the morgue, although I have learned to roll with surprises, taking them generally in my stride. But tonight had been almost too much.

Was my cover blown or wasn't it? The man lying in the alley knew my real name. But if he had worked with the man in San Francisco, and had talked with him before the bath, then my name could have been transmitted. Adding that up with the fact that here in Tokyo I was going under the name Carstens, and someone somewhere would have figured out that I was some sort of an undercover man.

But that still did not answer my question. Did they know who I was, and who I worked for?

A police cruiser turned the corner about two and a half blocks away on the opposite side of the street from me and came my way. I slouched low in my seat and waited for its lights to pass. A few moments later I looked up and the police car's red tail lights were going around the alleyway behind the morgue. I slammed the car in gear, roared out into the street and headed away as fast as the Honda could go. Had the police been tipped off? If so, by whom? But more importantly, had my car been spotted? I had evidently been set up. It was the only way the third man could have known to wait outside for me and the only way the cops could have come when they did. That meant one of two possibilities with an unlikely third.

Either someone had seen me at the morgue earlier in the afternoon, had put two and two together and realized that I would be back, or someone who was an extremely effective tail had been following me.

The unlikely third possibility was that there was an informer within the AXE Tokyo office. But the only person who knew I was going to the morgue tonight was Taffy. That she was the mole, which is the trade term for counterspy, I could not believe. But it was a possibility.

Some of the other things she had said and done over the past couple of days came to mind now, as well, and made me feel suddenly very uneasy.

First, in the hotel room, she had known that something like the elevator crash was going to happen. How?

Second, on the way out to her uncle's she had steered me down a dead end dirt road that our pursuers evidently knew quite well, and when they were almost on top of us, she had tried to hold me back and almost got me killed. Why?

Third, her initial insistence that I not go snooping around the morgue tonight was unlike her. Why?

I shook my head and chuckled. Although more unlikely persons than her had been detected as moles before, too many things were pointing in her direction—things for which she had ready explanations. She was becoming too obvious. It was almost like I was watching an old "whodunit" movie where at first everyone suspected the butler for obvious reasons. It never failed that the butler was not the culprit. And I could just not bring myself to believe that Taffy was the mole. But I was professional enough to know that like it or not, I would have to watch her closely for the next few days.

It was about four o'clock when I finally arrived back at Taffy's house, making doubly sure that no one was following me. If someone was back there tailing me he was damned good—better than anything I had ever seen or heard about, which all but eliminated at least one of the possibilities.

I knocked softly at her apartment door, and a few moments later Taffy's voice asked who it was.

"It's me," I whispered loudly.

The door opened and I brushed past her into the apartment. She locked the door behind me, then followed me into the living room where I turned on one of the lights.

She came into my arms. "Nick . . . darling. I was worried," she said, her head on my shoulder.

"Someone was there. Waiting for me," I said, carefully choosing my words.

She stiffened and looked up into my eyes. "Are you all right?" she said, genuine concern in her eyes and voice.

I nodded. "I had to kill all three of them. They were looking through the elevator operator's belongings."

"And?"

I hesitated only a moment, and then my earlier doubts dissolved. If she was the mole, she was good—almost too good. I believed her. "I need your help with something," I said.

"Anything, Nick. What is it?"

We parted and I pulled out the four white shawls, including the bloodied one from the dead elevator operator. When she saw them her eyes widened.

"I found these on the three men I had to kill tonight," I said, then held up the bloodied one. "This one the elevator operator put around his head just before he pulled the plug."

She stepped back away from the shawls as I held them out to her, an almost horrified expression on her face.

"What is it?" I said, stepping forward. "What are these things? What the hell do they mean?"

"Hachimakis," she stammered. "They are Hachimakis."

The word meant nothing to my limited Japanese vocabulary, but it evidently meant something to Taffy, and for an instant my doubts were back again, until she explained.

"They are ceremonial prayer shawls," she said after a moment. Then she shrugged and smiled weakly as she stepped to me and took the shawls. "You frightened me for a moment. These brought back some pretty powerful memories. They would for any Japanese who could remember, or had been told about the war."

"I'm still in the dark," I said. We moved to the couch where we sat down next to each other. "What do these have to do with the war?"

Taffy set all but one of the white shawls down on the couch beside her, and spread the fourth one out across our laps. It was about four feet long and only seven or eight inches wide, but for the first time I noticed that the material had been stitched in regular rows up and down the shawl. I ran my fingers over the tiny bumps.

"There are exactly one thousand stitches on each of these," she said. "And each stitch represents a prayer for the wearer to more easily enter heaven upon death," she said. "A few hundred years ago these were worn by the Samurai, but during the war these were worn by all Kamikaze pilots. Without these, the pilots would never have given their lives by crashing their airplanes into enemy ships or installations. Without these they would never have made it into heaven."

I sat back on the couch, the mist that had surrounded my thinking about this case suddenly clearing as if a fog was lifting in the morning sun. There was little doubt in my mind now that the Japanese terrorists who had crashed those four passenger planes had been wearing these shawls. And now the elevator operator and his friends turned up with them.

"The Kamikaze," I said suddenly, turning to her. "What happened to them after the war?"

She looked at me questioningly. "I don't understand what you mean, Nick."

"Surely all of the pilots who were in the Kamikaze

Corps during the war weren't killed. Some of them must have survived to be captured. What happened to those men?"

She shook her head. "I don't know. I suppose they may have been placed in POW camps until the occupation was completed and then later released along with the other soldiers captured." She got a faraway look in her eyes. "They were mostly young boys, Nick. And I am sure they were very idealistic."

"So?" I said almost too harshly. A lot of what I would be doing in the next few days on this case could depend heavily upon what she would tell me.

"I'm sure many of them committed *hari kari* rather than be captured, or later returned to their homes. It would have been a great dishonor for them to return to the living."

It was my turn to look at her questioningly, and she reached out and touched my arm.

"Poor Nick . . . darling. You are in a land where honor is above everything else. Unless you keep that constantly in the back of your mind you will never be able to understand us . . . the Japanese people." She looked away again.

"They were young and idealistic, and when they enlisted in the Kamikaze Corps it was with the knowledge that they would never return. Just after their enlistment, mass funerals were held for entire squadrons. They were already dead in the eyes of their countrymen. They had to be. At any moment, day or night they could be sent on a one-way assignment, so they had to be prepared for their deaths. Their wills had to be made out, they had to make their final preparations with their families and they had to say their last goodbyes to their sweethearts."

"It sounds gruesome," I said, and then I bit my lip. I was being insensitive.

"Not at all, Nick," Taffy said with fervor. "I was told by my mother and uncles that it was a beautiful ceremony. The families all were there, and instead of just looking at the ashes of their dead sons, they could talk with them, be with them and celebrate their ascent into heaven. And after that they were like gods, above all earthly concerns and laws. Nothing was too good for them. They were already dead. And this...," she said as she held up the shawl, "was their key to heaven."

What in hell was I up against, I wondered as I sat back once more in the soft cushions of the couch. These people, whoever they were, obviously were highly organized to be able to trace my movements with such thoroughness. But more dangerous than that were their beliefs, or as Taffy had put it, their idealism. Apparently, they were all ready to die to the man. And in order for me to get more information on what and where they were, and what their purpose was—if indeed they had a purpose other than terrorism—I would sooner or later have to capture one of them alive.

And that, I told myself wryly, would be no easy task.

I turned once again to Taffy who was studying my face. This was the last time I would test her, I thought. If she passed this one, I would be completely convinced that she was not the leak. But if she failed it ... I let that thought trail off.

Without giving a hint that what I was about to say was anything more or less important than the other things I had asked her, I formed my words carefully, watching her eyes which for me have always been telltale indicators of truth or fiction.

"Who or what is Aki Shintu?"

Without a flicker of her eyes she thought a moment, then shook her head. "I have no idea, Nick," she said.

CHAPTER TEN

Kazuka Akiyama had evidently arrived moments before Taffy and me, because she had just hung up her coat on the rack and was turning toward her desk when we entered the Amalgamated Press offices. For the benefit of the few legitimate newsmen around the counter, Taffy showed me to Kazuka's desk and loudly introduced us.

"Mr. Carstens, this is Miss Akiyama. I'm sure she will be able to help you with your new account."

Kazuka bowed and smiled. "Pleased to meet you, Mr. Carstens," she said to me, then she turned to Taffy. "Are you still on that assignment or are you free to work here this morning? We could use you."

Taffy turned questioningly toward me, but I nodded for her to go ahead. If this was anything like most other AXE offices the world round, it was understaffed. Taffy was most likely the only cryp, and would be desperately needed. I was sure than in her absence any number of urgent dispatches that needed coding had piled up.

When Taffy left us, promising to meet me downstairs at noon, Kazuka turned to me. "What can we do for you this morning?"

"Is there somewhere we can talk in private, Miss Akiyama," I said pleasantly.

"Of course," she said, and she led me to the same bug-proof conference room I had used earlier to send my message to Hawk. When the door was secured, and the green light winked on indicating that no clandestine monitoring devices were in operation, we dropped the pretenses.

"What's up, Nick?" she said, concerned. "Taffy was worried about you last night when you didn't show after your meeting with Hawk."

100

"I suppose I should have called in," I apologized. "But I was a little tied up."

She nodded and smiled, but asked nothing more about my activities the night before, and I was grateful for that. Not only was Kazuka beautiful, she was bright.

"I need to see Owen's office, and his files. I've got to find out what he was working on during the past few weeks or so before he called me, and then came out to San Francisco."

"That won't be too easy, I'm afraid," she said pursing her lips.

"Why?"

"Owen hardly ever kept notes or records of any kind on his assignments until each case was completed. He always said that if there was a mole around here, it would get no information on what he was working on from his files, only past history."

The word "mole" shot through my mind, and I was about to ask her if Owen, too, had his doubts about the security of this office, but then I thought better of it. There was also the possibility that Kazuka herself was the informer. But I seriously doubted it, although I knew that if Hawk were here he would say that was a definite sign of my weakness for beautiful women. And weaknesses of any kind, he would undoubtedly say, usually prove to be fatal for a Killmaster.

"I'd like to try anyway, Kazuka," I said.

She nodded, and led me out of the room and down a short corridor into a plain, almost sterile office. Only one desk, a couple of chairs, a typewriter on a stand and one file cabinet occupied the otherwise barren room. No photographs, paintings or even calendars were on the walls, nor was there anything other than a plain yellow tablet, a couple of pencils and a telephone on his desk.

I turned to Kazuka, the question mark in my mind evidently plain on my face, because she smiled and nodded.

"I told you. No records. I don't think you'll find much of anything in here that will help you."

I shrugged. "It's worth a try," I said. "Mind helping me? You know more about what he might have been working on in the past so that I won't pick up any false leads."

"Of course," she said, closing the door behind her. She flipped on the light switch and a green light above the door winked on a moment later. This room also had been bug-proofed.

"I'll take the desk, and you can have the file cabinet. When we're done we can switch and start all over again. We won't miss anything that way," I said.

For nearly two hours Kazuka and I worked, going through Owen's appointment books and schedules, coded message files, assignment charts, material and personnel requisitions and all the other paperwork my friend had kept over the past few years. But every bit of the paperwork had all been done in the past tense. Nothing was there that would indicate what he was working on just before he had come to San Francisco. Even the message he had sent to Hawk indicating he would be coming to the States to see me, and the travel vouchers for the trips to Hiroshima Taffy said he had taken, were not in the files. And that bothered me.

Kazuka was sitting in one of the chairs and I was perched on the edge of the desk when I finally came to the conclusion that Kazuka might be right.

"Nothing," I said. "But there has to be something. What about his message to Hawk on the Stateside trip? Where is that?"

Kazuka smiled tiredly. "Like I said, Nick, it was all kept up here. . . ." She tapped her temple with one finger.

"What about the message sheets themselves?"

"Owen insisted that no copies be kept. He would write out the message and would usually code it himself. Then he would destroy all copies of his message as well as the decoded reply after he had memorized them both. Later, after he had completed the assignment, he always took a day or two to re-write all the messages, vouchers and other paperwork just for the files."

I had to smile. It was neat. And yet he had been dis-covered somehow, and killed. There had to be something here to point in the direction he had been going. Some-thing. Anything.

The telephone on the desk rang softly, and Kazuka picked it up. "Yes?" she said.

A moment later. "No, you can handle that yourself. I'll be in conference here for a little while yet."

She hung up the phone and looked up at me. "It was nothing much," she said. "We do have to run a real press operation here as well as our other work. That was just one of our member newspapers with a bitch about the service. One of the front men can handle. . . ."

But I was not hearing her at that moment, and she stopped talking in mid-sentence. The telephone. Of course.

I jumped off the desk. "Did Owen ever use the phone? For outside calls, I mean?" I asked excitedly.

Her eyes narrowed. "Of course he did, Nick, but I don't see. . . ."

"Those calls," I said, interrupting her. "Did they have to go through the switchboard here?"

"Yes," she said, nodding.

"Okay now. Are records of any kind kept?" I asked, and she suddenly saw what I was driving at.

"Of course," she said, jumping up and smiling. "Wait here."

She hurried out of the room, and was gone for about five minutes. I lit one of my specially made cigarettes and when I was half finished with it she barged back into the office lugging two large, looseleaf books which she plopped down on the desk.

"These are the records of the incoming and outgoing calls. One book for each. Today's calls are on loose sheets, and won't be posted in these books until tomor-row."

"How far back do these go?" I said, stubbing out my cigarette, then stuffing the butt in my coat pocket.

She smiled. "You're learning."

"Hawk chewed me out the last time I left one of these here, and I don't relish the thought of another session like that."

"I don't think I'd care for the pleasure of that kind of meeting," she said, and then she turned her attention back to the telephone logs. "These go back to the first of the year, and will be used to the end of this year. One year per book since this office was opened."

I pulled the other chair around to the side of the desk, shoved the incoming call book over to her, and opened to the first page of the outgoing book.

On each line were listed two times—one for the beginning of the call and one for the end of the call—the extension number doing the calling, the number called and in most cases the person or firm called as well as the city and country. On a few of the lines here and there in the first part of the book, however, that information had not been included, only the number and the times listed.

"What does this mean?" I said, turning the book around so Kazuka could see it, and pointing to one such call.

"That was most likely a call to a blind number," she said. "Probably to one of our field people."

"Isn't this a little dangerous?" I said. "Anyone could be monitoring these calls."

"In theory, yes," Kazuka said, nodding, "but in practice not likely. We keep pretty tight watch on the lines. But all such calls are kept very short, and are always in a code of one kind or another. So it really isn't too bad."

I pulled the book back to me, noting from the phone on the desk that Owen's extension was one-seven, and I began searching through the telephone log, starting on a date that was two weeks before he had telephoned me.

On that first day, Owen had made five long-distance blind calls, as well as a few routine calls to member newspapers in the Tokyo area.

I jotted down all the blind numbers and dates, and flipped the page to the next day.

On the second day, Owen had made three more long-distance blind calls, and on the third day, seven more. Each day after that he had made any number of blind calls from three on one Sunday to as many as seventeen two days before he called me.

Abruptly, the day before he telephoned me, the calls stopped. The next day his call to me in San Francisco was listed, and after that nothing for one-seven.

Kazuka had finished before me, and when I looked up she shook her head. "Not much luck here," she said. "Only routine incoming calls. How about you?"

I pushed the tablet on which I had jotted down the numbers across to her. "In the two weeks before he telephoned me he made more than a hundred blind calls."

Kazuka looked in disbelief at the long list of numbers. "One or two blind calls a month would be unusual. But this," she said and looked at me. "What could it mean?"

"I don't know, but I think once we find out who belongs to all those numbers, we might have a pretty good idea just what Owen was up to."

"This could take weeks."

"We don't have weeks. How about the staff? Can you get them on it without telling them what it's for, and without arousing too much suspicion?"

"Maybe," she said hesitantly, but then she nodded. "Yes, I can. We'll stay the night. I'll tell them it's a hush-hush project for one of our member newspapers. We'll have it done by morning."

"You're a doll," I said. I quickly scribbled out a message to Hawk and handed it to her. "Top priority," I said, then got up from the desk. I looked at my watch; it was noon. "Have to run. Promised Taffy I'd take her to lunch."

"Isn't that a little dangerous?" she said. "I mean after what happened at the hotel, and what you ran into last night?"

"Nothing happened last night," I lied, suddenly very much on guard.

She laughed. "I read the papers, Nick. This morning's headlines were about some character whose throat was slit. They found him last night at the back entrance to the city morgue. No clues." She looked at me, her eyes twinkling. "I'm not the mole if there is one and if that's what you're thinking. But I'm not stupid either. That is the same morgue in which the elevator operator's body is being kept."

I had to laugh with her, not so much at her deductive reasoning which was fantastic, but more at myself for seeing bogey men behind every tree.

"Okay, sweetheart," I said lightly. "I'm going to lunch now, but it's business. Let's just call it a hunting trip. But code this message to Hawk yourself, and get it sent out right away if you can. It's important."

She nodded, then stood up and squeezed my arm. "Be careful, Nick. Owen was a damned good man—but not good enough."

"And you loved him," I said impulsively, instantly regretting my words.

She lowered her eyes. "Yes," she said quietly. "We were to be married in two months."

"I'm sorry. I didn't know," I said. I reached over and kissed her on the cheek. "I'll be careful because I want to be around when this thing is wrapped up. I'll buy you a drink, and we can go out someplace quiet for dinner."

She looked up after a long moment, a weak smile on her face. "It's a date," she said.

I stopped halfway out the door, and turned back. "One last thing," I said, and Kazuka looked at me. "The words Aki Shintu—do they mean anything to you?"

She thought a moment and then shook her head. "No, should they?"

"I don't know," I said thoughtfully. "See what you can find out about it, would you?"

"Sure, Nick," she said, and then I went downstairs to meet Taffy.

CHAPTER ELEVEN

Women have always been a large part of my life, and keeping their emotions as well as my own under control. But now as I glanced at Taffy sitting across the table from me I could not help but compare her with Kazuka—and Taffy was coming out second best.

I smiled, and wondered briefly what Hawk would say if he knew what I was thinking at this moment. Taffy caught the gesture.

"I don't think anything is funny," she said nervously. "We're sitting ducks here."

I looked up at the Ginza crowd surging past where we sat at a sidewalk cafe table, then back down at her. "Exactly," I said. "I want to be a sitting duck."

Her eyes narrowed. "What the hell did you and Kazuka talk about all morning?" she said peevishly.

I laughed out loud. Jealousy. This was getting to be too much, and although I no longer suspected Taffy as being the mole, if there was one, I was finding myself becoming a little bored with her sometimes demanding attitudes.

"Business," I said. "Nothing but business, which is why we are here."

"You're going to end up dead before you find out what's going on if you keep this up," she said.

I shook my head. "Not here. It would attract too much attention, something I don't think they'd risk yet."

"They?" Taffy said, sitting forward, a new interest on her face. "What did you and Kazuka find?"

"Nothing much," I said. "But since that attempt in the elevator they've had plenty of chances to kill me. They haven't, not even at the morgue. No. There's something else here. Maybe it's only a gut feeling, but I'm sure they're just watching me for now. Waiting. If I get too close, they'll do something."

"That doesn't make any sense," she snapped.

For a moment I had to agree with her, because up to this point the things I had just said to her had only been vague thoughts in my mind, and I had taken the thinking no further. But then it struck me.

"Sure it does," I said.

She looked closely at me, but said nothing.

"Look, Taffy," I said excitedly. "I brought us down here as sitting ducks, just like you said. But I wanted someone to take a pot shot at us. I figured they'd most likely miss and I could run down whoever tried. But that's not going to happen. They'll follow us all right, and unless we stumble onto something, that's all they'll do. Now. Doesn't that tell you something?"

She shook her head, a confused expression on her face. "I don't see. . . ."

I cut her off. "Of course," I said. "They're working on some kind of a time limit. Whatever it is they're planning will happen soon. At first, when I showed up here in Tokyo, they were frightened. Thought I was on to them. But then later they realized that I was just making stabs in the dark, so I wasn't any real threat. But if they killed me now, there would be an all-out investigation, which might spoil their plans, whatever those plans might be."

"Assuming you're right," Taffy said slowly and carefully, "what sort of people are we dealing with? And just what is this plan you're talking about?"

I thought a moment, some of the jumble of yesterday beginning to clear in my mind. When I looked up she was watching me closely.

"We know one thing for sure," I began, "and that is that we are dealing with fanatics. Kamikazes. People who don't care if they die for their cause, which makes them doubly dangerous and doubly elusive."

I tried to bring some order to my next thoughts. "Whatever their plan or mission is, it's important enough to have the backing of someone quite intelligent and extremely capable, otherwise they would not have been able to trace my movements through this city so well. And whoever the leader or leaders are, they must be ruthless, otherwise there would not be so much dedication in the men who have already died."

So far so good, I told myself. But what about the mission? "And their mission," I said smoothly without pausing, "has something to do with the last four commercial air disasters—Owen's included—over a three or four month span. In each case Japanese men were involved who were trained pilots and willing to die."

Taffy nodded. "That was the information Hawk brought to you?"

"Right," I said.

"So, I'm *still* in the dark. What are you planning to do?"

"Catch a Kamikaze," I said as I got up from the table, grabbed her arm and propelled her out into the press of human traffic flowing smoothly along the wide sidewalk.

"Where are we going?" she demanded as we moved quickly away from the sidewalk cafe, several surprised people looking our way.

"The best way to catch a tail is by trying to shake him, but ineptly," I snapped. "Now be quiet and just follow me."

Taffy glanced back over her shoulder, and then we hurried along in the direction the crowd was moving.

We walked in a generally large circle bounded by the huge Ginza shopping and entertainment district, never leaving the press of the crowds, but switching back and ducking down narrow side streets without a pattern. It wasn't until we had been going steadily for more than two hours before I caught my first glimpse of a small black, Suburu sedan with two men in it. And from that moment on I was sure we had our tail.

Fifteen minutes later, when we were again on the main avenue which runs the length of the Ginza, I saw the same black Suburu, only now there were two different men in it, which meant we had at least two men tailing us on foot. Evidently they were switching off every so often, so that if we spotted someone on foot in the crowd once, we might not see them again.

It was smooth. Very smooth. But if my plan was going to work, we were going to have to ditch that car, at least for a few minutes.

Two blocks later I found what I was looking for. Earlier we had passed this extremely narrow alleyway—too narrow even for the Suburu—and now it was going to be perfect for what I wanted.

I stopped and pretended to examine the cloth goods in the window of a small shop next to the alley, and Taffy suddenly seemed nervous.

"We've got our tail," I said quietly, but with a broad smile on my face.

Taffy started to look wildly around, but I yanked on her arm, pulling her around to the window.

"But we'll blow it if you keep that up," I snapped, still smiling for the benefit of our watchers.

"Where?" she whispered urgently.

"Two men in a small black car about a half a block back, and somewhere two men on foot," I said.

"We'd better get out of here, Nick," she said, frightened.

"No way. We've got them now," I said.

"But there're four of them. . . ," she started to protest.

"Only two when we go down this alley," I said, nodding slightly. "The car won't be able to follow us."

She was about to protest again when I shoved her sharply toward the alley. "Now," I said, and we pushed through the crowd down the narrow space between the buildings.

As far as I could tell, this alley continued for about two blocks until it opened on the Avenue of Shintu, another of the main thoroughfares in this district. The men in the Suburu would now be speeding the several blocks around to where the alley exited, and would be waiting for us. But I was not going to be there.

About a hundred yards down the alley, I shoved Taffy into a darkened doorway, and pressed into the confined space with her. A moment later, two men dressed in conventional Japanese costumes emerged from the crowd behind us, searching frantically ahead of them in our direction. My tails.

I jumped from the doorway, leaving the startled Taffy behind, and in a few quick steps caught up to the men who suddenly realized they had been spotted.

One of them suddenly had a gun in his hand, and as it came up toward me, I flicked my wrist and Hugo snapped comfortably into my palm. In one quick, smooth motion I sliced up and across the man's belly, and for a long, ago- nizing moment everything around me seemed to stop. But then the man dropped the gun and both hands went to his sliced-open stomach from which his intestines were sliding out onto the street, while the second man bolted toward the main avenue.

Everything seemed to be working in slow motion, and in three or four steps I had caught up to the other man, and had tapped him lightly on the head just behind his right ear. He fell hard, but was unconscious and still alive.

Taffy reached me as I was heaving the man's inert form to its feet, supporting him like I would support a drunken friend. The crowd had suddenly gathered around the first man, whose dying moans had finally stopped. Dead or not, he would not be saying much about me, I figured as I hurried toward the main street at the opposite end of the alley from where I was sure the Suburu was waiting.

"My God, Nick what are you doing?" Taffy shouted as we emerged onto the wide sidewalk.

"Shut up," I snapped urgently. All I needed now was for her shouting to attract enough attention for a cop. I would have a hard time explaining what I was doing with an unconscious man over my shoulder and a dead one in the alley.

A moment later a taxi slowly came down the street and I waved it over to us.

We piled in the car, keeping the unconscious man between us, and I gave the cabby an address a block behind Taffy's apartment building. When the cabby looked at the man between us, and then up at me, I smiled and shrugged.

"Only afternoon, and already he has had too much to drink," I said.

The cabby studied my face for a moment, but then he nodded and smiled and turned forward and we were speeding away from the alley.

By the time the men in the Suburu realized something was wrong and came down the alley on foot to investigate, we would be long gone.

Twenty minutes later we pulled up at the address I had given the cabby. I paid the fare, and between Taffy and me we managed to get the still unconscious man out of the cab and into the vestibule of an apartment house.

The cabby remained parked at the curb as he watched us drag the man up the stairs and inside, but once the door was closed he was apparently satisfied that we were not up to anything funny, and he pulled away.

Fortunately no one was in the hallway, and as far as we knew, no one saw us emerge from the building a few moments after we entered, our unconscious friend still in tow.

It took us a full fifteen minutes to go around the long block, and make it up the back stairs into Taffy's apartment. During that time she said nothing to me, but once inside, she exploded.

"Dammit, Nick, do you know what you might have done?" she shouted.

"Don't worry about it," I said as I laid the man on the floor in the living room, but I was only half hearing her objections. The corner of a white prayer shawl sticking out of the man's pocket claimed my undivided attention. I withdrew it. It was exactly the same kind of shawl the others had been carrying. I had been right in my assumptions back at the sidewalk cafe. But Taffy was continuing with her tirade.

"We could have been killed, Nick. Or maybe stopped by the police. What would we have told them?" she said, her voice raising in pitch.

"Look," I said sharply, catching her off guard, "you said you wanted to help with this, so don't go soft on me now. We're too damned close."

She started to say something else, but then evidently changed her mind, and fell silent.

I turned back to our guest, and in a few moments I had his hands and feet trussed up together behind his back with the prayer shawl. This one was not going to die on me, not if I could help it, and not before I had a chance to ask him a few questions.

Quickly searching him to make sure he had no weapons other than the .38 I found stuck in an inner pocket, I came up empty-handed. Surely if this man was as much the fanatic as the others, he would not leave to chance his getting captured and rendered unable to take his own life without the gun.

As he was coming slowly awake, I held open his slack jaw and quickly examined his teeth. Once before I had lost a man who had a cyanide pellet concealed in a false tooth. But as far as I could tell, this man was carrying no such self-destructive device.

I sat back on the floor and watched as he started to come to. Taffy sat down on the low couch across the room from us, but said nothing. She looked hurt by what I had said to her, and I made a mental note to apologize when this was all over.

The man finally came fully awake and for the first few seconds struggled violently against his bonds, but then he slumped on the floor, turning his head so he could see Taffy and then turning back to me.

"Why were you following me?" I asked, but it was as if

the man could not hear, because he turned away from me to study the paintings on the opposite wall.

I reached out and yanked his head around. "Who sent you?" I snapped.

The man just glared at me, but said nothing, the only hint that he was frightened was his shallow, rapid breathing.

I reached behind him and yanked on the prayer shawl I had him tied up with. "Your *Hachimaki,* what does it. . . ," I began, but the man's eyes bulged nearly out of their sockets, and his face turned red with rage as he violently jerked away from my grasp. I had hit a nerve.

"Aki Shintu," I said softly to him, a slow smile spreading across my face. "Who or what is that?"

I had evidently said something wrong, because his features suddenly relaxed, a sigh escaped from his lips and he lay still. At first I thought he was dead, but then his eyes blinked and he smiled at me.

I have never believed in torture of any kind, as much of it as I have seen and as much of it that has been inflicted on me. But I am a realist who knows that under some extreme conditions, it is the only way to make a man talk.

"You are going to tell me about Aki Sintu," I said, "and very soon."

I moved around behind the man, grabbed his ring finger in my right hand, and slowly began to bend it upward toward the back of his hand. He stiffened up.

"Aki Shintu," I repeated. "Tell me." I bent the finger back even farther, and it turned white. The man's entire body had gone rigid now, but he made no sounds, even though the pain must have been unbelievable.

"One more time," I said, holding the pressure on the finger steady. "Aki Shintu. Tell me."

The man said nothing.

I bent the finger farther back and suddenly it snapped, the bone breaking through the skin. The man jerked violently, and I turned away sickened at what I had done.

But if need be, I told myself, I would continue breaking his fingers until he talked.

Taffy's scream caused me to snap around in time to see a gush of blood spreading out in front of the man's head. I jumped over the body as his eyes rolled up into the back of his head, and his breath whistled from his lungs past the remnants of his tongue which he had completely bitten through. In a very few moments he would be dead, I knew. He would bleed to death or choke on his own blood. And now it was too late. Even if he did want to tell me anything he could not. Not without a tongue.

It was the only way in which he could commit suicide, and now my estimation of the men I was dealing with went up a hundred percent, and for the first time I began to wonder if I was going to be able to solve this case at all against these odds.

CHAPTER TWELVE

It was nearly midnight by the time I had telephoned Kazuka at Amalgamated Press, explained my problem and she had located and sent out two men to take care of the body. They would ask no questions, she assured me, nor would they say anything to anyone. They were trusted men.

When they were gone with the body, Taffy and I spent almost an hour cleaning the blood off the floor, and then we fell into bed, both of us drifting off to sleep immediately.

The luminous hands on my wristwatch were pointing to six o'clock when I got up to answer the telephone, still groggy from less than four hours of sleep. It was Kazuka who had spent the night at the office.

"Nick, I've got that information you wanted," she said guardedly.

"Right," I said glancing down at Taffy who was just beginning to stir. "We'll be there in a few minutes."

By the time I had finished my shower, Taffy was up and dressed, and we left together in her car for the fifteen-minute drive to the office through the almost deserted streets. Only a few people were up and around at this hour, but soon the streets would again be choked with humanity, as the business day began.

Kazuka was waiting alone in the outer office when we arrived, and she looked disheveled; her hair in disarray, her clothes rumpled and her eyes red-rimmed.

"I sent the others home as soon as they were done," she said to me, as she led us back to the secure conference room. "Only one teletype operator is here now, and he's busy finishing up the morning reports."

Once in the room Kazuka turned to me with an odd expression on her face. "We may have hit the jackpot, Nick," she said. "At least it feels that way, but I can't make any sense of it."

"What did you find out?" I asked.

We sat down around the conference table and Kazuka pushed a sheaf of papers across to me. Taffy looked over my shoulder.

Each sheet of paper contained a portion of the telephone numbers Owen had called during the couple of weeks before his ill-fated trip to the States. Behind each phone number was a person's name and location.

Quickly scanning the several pages of names and numbers, the only pattern I could discern was that Owen had telephoned practically every major city in the world. A few minutes later I looked up questioningly at Kazuka.

"Who are these people?" I asked.

"AXE contacts," Kazuka said. "And that's about all I can tell you about them. Mostly they're secret runners or observers for us. Most of them think they are working part-time for Amalgamated Press and not AXE, but they all are being paid to keep tabs on local situations, and keep their mouths shut. We tell them it's because of the competition—which it is in a way."

I looked back down at the list, somewhat disappointed. I had hoped for something a little more concrete than this.

"There is something a little odd about those calls, though," Kazuka said thoughtfully.

"I looked up at her. "What do you mean?"

"I don't know if it makes any sense, but I ran the list through our small office computer here, trying to find some pattern. I got the answer back just a few minutes ago."

"Go on," I said. Almost anything would help.

"The only pattern is that those calls were made to every major city in the world in every country except Germany, Italy and here in Japan. The only exception to that is Hiroshima."

I had to think about that for a moment. Instead of clearing up the puzzle, this bit of information was making things worse.

"Owen never called any contact men in Germany, or Italy. You sure of that?"

Kazuka shrugged. "If he did, he didn't make the calls through our switchboard. I also checked the logs further back, but there was nothing for those countries. Nor did Owen call contacts in any cities here in Japan except for Hiroshima. And he called that number half a dozen times."

Hiroshima. That city kept cropping up again and again. Something evidently very important was happening there. So important Owen not only made half a dozen calls, but he made a couple of trips there. And just after his last trip, he was murdered. That was my next step.

Taffy spoke up for the first time since we had arrived. "Have you got the name and address for the Hiroshima contact?" she asked Kazuka.

"Right. It's on the list there," Kazuka said, looking at me.

I flipped the pages until I came to the first Hiroshima number, after which was listed a man's name and an address. "Who is this man? Do you know him?"

"I've only heard of him," Kazuka said. "Shoban Hobi is just another of our contact men. I've never issued him a large check for services, but he has been steady."

"Reliable?"

"As far as I know," Kazuka said.

"I'm going to see him," I said. "Today."

"I'll come with you," Taffy said.

I looked at her and shook my head. "No way, not with the kind of people we're dealing with. I'd feel a lot better if you stayed behind. They won't bother you here, but if you're with me. . . ."

"I don't care," Taffy said obstinately. "I'm going with you."

"We do need you here," Kazuka said, and Taffy snapped around to glare at her, but she said nothing.

"This is my job, Taffy," I said as gently as possible. "I know you're upset about Owen, but it would be better if you remained here and caught up with the workload."

She seemed to hesitate for a moment, then she slumped back in her chair. "All right," she said. "You win."

"Which reminds me," I said, turning back to Kazuka. "Anything back from Hawk yet?"

Kazuka handed across a message flimsy. "Came in about three this morning. Figured it could wait until you came in."

The message was short and to the point, confirming what I had suspected. Investigations showed that in the air crash in which Owen had died and in one of the crashes in Europe, the Japanese terrorists had been carrying white shawls that so far had been unidentified. The remains from the other two crashes had been too badly burned for any positive identification of clothing. But it was enough to convince me that I had been right. The same organization that had involved nearly a dozen men so far here in Tokyo, also was involved with the air crashes.

"How about Aki Shintu?" I asked after a long pause. "Did you find anything on that?"

Kazuka's brows knitted. "I don't know what you've gotten yourself into Nick, but whatever it is it sure is taking some strange twists."

"You found something?" I said, sitting forward.

She nodded. "Aki Shintu, or more accurately Colonel Aki Shintu, was Chief of Operations for a group of Kamikaze Squadrons in Southern Honshu just before the war ended."

It was like a slot machine suddenly coming up all cherries. "He disappeared after the war. He was presumed dead. His body was never found." I said it all in a rush.

Kazuka nodded dumbfounded and I continued a little more slowly. "And you're going to tell me he was from Hiroshima," I said, but Kazuka shook her head.

"He may have been, but the records were unclear about that. It did say, though, that his operations base was just outside of Hiroshima."

"Was he married? Did he have any family?" I asked.

"I don't know," Kazuka said, and I turned to Taffy.

"Have you ever heard of this Colonel?" I asked.

"I told you before I hadn't," Taffy said. "He was probably not very important otherwise I'm sure I would have learned about him. But I never saw his name in any books I've read."

"She's right," Kazuka interjected. "I don't think he was very important. At least the records we've turned up show him as just a minor officer, who commanded only for a few months near the end of the war. Then, after the atomic bombing of Nagasaki and Hiroshima, he disappeared. Probably committed suicide. A lot of them did then."

I shook my head. "No, he didn't. Unless I miss my mark completely, he's still alive and kicking, and very probably behind this entire mess."

"That's a little hard to believe, Nick," Kazuka said. "At the end of the war he was in his mid-forties, which would make him nearly eighty years old now. Even if he is around, he couldn't do much harm."

"More than a dozen men may have died for him so far," I said.
"And I'd bet almost anything that he is the mastermind behind this entire scheme, whatever the scheme is."

"Which leaves you with two questions," Kazuka said.

I said nothing, waiting for her to continue.

"First of all, what are they planning, and second of all, why?"

I nodded. "That's why I'm going to Hiroshima. I'd like to have a little chat with Colonel Shintu."

By nine o'clock the office had filled up for business as usual, and Kazuka had arranged a commercial flight for me to Hiroshima for early that evening. All flights before that time were solidly booked, and I did not want to go out to the airport and wait for the off chance someone would not show up and I could fly space available. Nor did I want to risk taking a military flight or chartering an airplane and pilot. Enough attention had already been centered on me, I did not want to attract any more.

Through the morning and into late afternoon, Taffy worked to catch up on the load of messages waiting to be sent Stateside, while I remained in the conference room once again going over all the material we had covered so far. But the files, telephone logs and history of this mysterious Colonel Sintu offered up no further clues, so that by five o'clock I was tired and no closer to the truth than I had at nine that morning.

Taffy was tied up with a string of incoming messages so Kazuka volunteered to drive me to Taffy's apartment for an overnight bag, and then out to the airport early, but she said she would have to get back within a couple of hours.

We drove most of the way in silence, but when we finally pulled off the highway onto the airport terminal road, she turned to me.

"Do you really think you'll find anything in Hiroshima, Nick?" she said.

I had been watching the countryside pass by and thinking about Owen, and her question startled me. "I don't know," I said.

"If that's where it's all happening, you'll undoubtedly get a warm reception," she said.

"I hope so," I countered. "I'd be a little disappointed if I didn't."

"Be careful, Nick," Kazuka said. Her eyes were bright and her face was animated. "I care about what happens to you. I don't want the same thing as Owen. . . ."

"Owen was a good man," I interrupted. "But I'm not

sure he knew what kind of people he was up against. I know."

We pulled up in front of the terminal building, and Kazuka parked the car. "I'll come in with you," she said. "That is, if that offer of a drink is still open."

I smiled and nodded. "Sure thing. I've got some time before my plane takes off."

We went into the busy terminal, and I checked in at the ticket counter for my reservation before we went to the cocktail lounge which overlooked the East-West runway, and sat at a corner table. I had the distinct feeling that we were being watched, but I could not spot our tail, if indeed we had one.

After our drinks had come, and we had settled down, I pushed the uneasy feeling aside as just paranoia. If they knew I was on my way to Hiroshima, which was doubtful, they would not bother watching me here. They would probably just await my arrival there, and then pick up my trail.

Kazuka was talking, and I turned my attention back to her.

"I'm sorry," I said. "I guess I was thinking about something else, and I kind of drifted off."

Kazuka smiled. "It wasn't important," she said, but she had a funny look in her eyes.

"Please," I said. "What were you saying?"

"I was asking you about Miss Nashima," she said softly.

"What about Taffy?" I asked.

"Are you . . . I mean do you love her?" she said hesitantly.

I was surprised at her bluntness. "No," I said. "She's just an old friend. I knew her when Owen and I were working together a few years ago." Was I telling her the truth, I wondered. Or did I really still have a feeling for Taffy?

Kazuka was blushing. "Look, Nick, I'm sorry I asked. I don't know what got into me."

I reached out and took her hand. "You don't trust her, do you?" I said.

Kazuka looked shocked, but she didn't say anything.

"I had my doubts too," I said seriously. "But if there is a leak anywhere, I don't think it's her."

"I hope you're right, Nick," she said, but she did not sound convinced.

Kazuka's words stayed with me, passing again and again through my mind during the five hundred mile flight from Tokyo to the southern tip of Honshu and the industrial city of Hiroshima.

Founded in 1594 on the Ota River Delta, Hiroshima had been a thriving industrial center of more than 300,-000 people when the war started. But all that had come to an abrupt halt when the United States dropped an atomic bomb on August 6, 1945 killing almost 150,000 people.

Since that time, however, the city had been mostly rebuilt and now its population was approaching the half million mark. Once again it had become one of Japan's major ports and industrial centers, and now possibly the center for some conspiracy that I was desperately trying to solve.

Colonel Aki Shintu was no doubt at the center of what was happening, but I could not come even close to figuring what role Taffy Nashima could be playing in this drama if she was a part of it. Kazuka's remark had caused many of my old doubts to reappear, and as we landed, I suddenly realized that for some reason I could not remember exactly what Taffy's face looked like. It was a forboding feeling.

No matter what happened here, I promised myself that as soon as I returned to Tokyo I was going to do a complete rundown on Taffy's background. One way or the other I was going to put my doubts about her to rest. I only hoped that whatever I found vindicated her.

Within half an hour I had collected my small suitcase, and was in a taxi heading into town toward the address for the AXE contact, Shoban Hobi.

I was hoping that he would be able to tell me what Owen had been working on down here so that I would have something tangible to go on, and with any luck, perhaps he'd have a clue as to why Owen had called so many AXE contacts all over the world, yet only one in Japan and none in Germany or Italy.

We were in a slum district of the city when the cabby slowed down and stopped behind a long line of cars. I glanced at my watch. It was nearly midnight.

"What's the problem?" I said, sitting forward in my seat.

"Looks like an accident up ahead, sir," the cabby said. "Police have the road blocked."

I peered ahead, and about half a block away I could see the blue flashing lights of several police cars, and what looked like an ambulance. My gut tightened.

"The address I gave you," I said to the cabby. "Is it anywhere near here?"

The cabby nodded. "Yes. It should be just about where the police cars are."

"Damn," I swore half under my breath. "Wait here for me," I snapped to the cabby and jumped out of the car and hurried down the line until I reached the small knot of people standing around.

A youngish looking man was laying face down in the middle of the street in a pool of blood. As I watched, the police were just finishing with their work, and the ambulance attendants loaded the dead man on a stretcher, placed a white sheet over him and took him away.

"What happened?" I asked in Japanese to an old man standing just in front of me.

The man turned slightly in my direction. "It is poor Shoban," the man said in a gravelly voice. "He fell from his window. Dead instantly."

"When?" I said, barely breathing the word.

The old man looked at me strangely. "Twenty minutes ago," he said.

I stepped back, and then turned and hurried back to the cab, jumped in the back seat and ordered the cabby to get the hell out of here.

"Where to, sir?" the confused cabby asked.

"A hotel. Any hotel, as long as it's downtown," I barked. It was time now for some serious thinking, some very serious thinking.

CHAPTER THIRTEEN

I stood looking out the window seven stories down to the street and the sparse nighttime traffic. Somewhere five hundred miles to the north was the informer, who could only be one of two persons: either Taffy Nashima or Kazuka Akiyama. Both of those women had access to Shoban Hobi's name and the knowledge that I was coming here to see him.

Both of them had easy access to all the information they needed to stop me, and yet as far as I could see neither of them had a motive strong enough to be involved with an organization that had caused Owen's death.

It was perplexing. Especially so because I knew that I had fond feelings for both of them.

One thing was certain, however, I told myself as I stepped away from the window. My usefulness here in Hiroshima was over before it had begun. With the death of Shoban there was little or nothing I could accomplish here.

No. My next step would have to be back in Tokyo where I would start a complete investigation of Taffy and Kazuka. If either of them were involved I would soon find out.

I laid down fully dressed on the bed facing the door, Wilhelmina in hand, to wait for the morning. The next plane north did not leave until nine and I wanted to get at least a little rest before I began the next stage of my investigations.

It seemed as if I had just sprawled on the bed and closed my eyes when there was a soft knocking on the door. I became instantly alert and sat up. The knocking had stopped and for a long moment in the darkness I wasn't sure I had heard it at all, but then it came again and Taffy's muffled voice called my name.

"Nick . . . Nick darling, are you in there?"

I jumped up from the bed and hurried to stand flat against the wall near the door. "Yes?" I said softly.

"My God, Nick—it's me . . . Taffy. Let me in," Taffy said urgently. She sounded out of breath.

I cautiously unlocked the door and stepped aside. "Come in," I said, and I raised my Luger to point directly at the door.

Taffy burst into the room, and when she saw me she ignored the upraised gun, gave a little cry and rushed into my arms, sobbing almost uncontrollably.

For a moment I kept my gun trained on the open door, ready for anyone who might be behind her, but we were alone, and I put my arms around her.

She babbled incoherently and cried for several long minutes, until I was finally able to calm her down sufficiently so that I could check the corridor and then lock the door.

She was sitting on the edge of the bed when I turned back to her, and it looked as if she had been crying for a long time.

"What's wrong?" I snapped. "What are you doing here?"

"They've got my mother," she cried.

"What?"

"They called me just after you left and said they had kidnapped my mother and would kill her unless I did what I was told."

My mind was spinning. Something was drastically wrong. "How did you get down here?" I asked, coming halfway across the room to her.

"They had an airplane," she said, and a wildness crept into her voice. "I was supposed to meet them at the Obi

Airways Hanger in Tokyo, but when I got there someone came up from behind and blindfolded me."

"You didn't see anyone?"

"No," she said, shaking her head. "They told me to be very quiet or my mother would die. I did what they told me."

"What happened then?" I asked.

"They took me somewhere in a car, and then brought me onto an airplane. It was a big one I think. Or at least it sounded big. They made me keep my blindfold on until we landed, and they drove me in another car downtown. I was told what hotel you were staying at and what room you were in, and then they just left me on the sidewalk. I waited a few minutes until they were gone, and they took off my blindfold, and walked here."

"Does anyone know you're here?" I asked.

"No," she said, and she looked deeply shaken. "I tried to call Kazuka at work, but they said she had gone home. There was no answer at her apartment when I called there. Nick, I was desperate. I didn't have any time. I had to do what they told me."

"All right," I said. "Take it easy. This just may work out after all." This was the most unlikely story I had ever heard in my life, especially in the way Taffy had tried to implicate Kazuka. But I had to admit that the story was no more odd than some of the things I had already been through on this case. There was still the possibility that Taffy was telling me the truth, in which case Kazuka was the mole, and was very possibly in Hiroshima at that moment.

"What do they want?" I asked, putting my Luger back in its holster.

Taffy looked wildly around the room, avoiding my eyes. "We can't do it, Nick. We can't . . . ," she trailed off weakly.

"What is it?" I said. "What did they tell you?"

"They said they would have a car waiting downstairs for us. You're supposed to come unarmed."

"Or else they'll kill your mother?"

She nodded miserably. "I didn't know what to do, Nick. They told me to somehow convince you to come with me. They said they just wanted to talk to you. But I can't."

"You just did," I said quietly. Trap or not, this was the first solid lead I had come across so far, and there was no way I was going to pass it up.

Taffy jumped up. "No . . . no, Nick, you can't. They'll kill you."

"And if you don't produce me, they'll kill your mother."

She looked deflated. "Yes," she whispered.

"Then let's go," I said. "It's the only way."

We left my room and went down the back stairs and stopped at the landing between the first and second floors. A grimy window overlooked the alley below, where a black Mercedes sedan was parked. I could not see if anyone was inside or not from this angle, and for a moment I had my doubts if what I was doing was the right thing.

If Taffy was telling the truth, her mother was in serious danger, and even if I went along with their demands, it was likely she would be killed anyway. But no matter what the truth was, I would be walking into a very dangerous situation. I would probably be signing my own death warrant.

"What's the matter?" Taffy said, breaking me out of my thoughts.

"I was just trying to get a look at who is in that car down there."

Taffy peered through the window and stiffened. "Nick, you'd better not. . . ."

"It's the only way," I said, finally making up my mind. Although I was being led into a trap, it was the only way in which I was going to get anywhere. When I discovered something, I would be able to play the situation by ear. It was not exactly the most orthodox method of investigation, but I've been in tougher spots and survived.

We went all the way downstairs and through the back door into the alleyway. Two men got out of the car, and without a word quickly frisked me, coming up with Wilhelmina and Hugo, but not Pierre my gas bomb.

One of the men opened the back door of the car for us, and in fifteen minutes we were speeding out of Hiroshima in the pre-dawn darkness.

Neither of the men spoke during the long ride, which ended down a long, narrow dirt road that came to an obviously abandoned air strip. An old DC3 painted military olive drab, but with its markings covered, was warming up at one end of the runway, and the driver headed the car in that direction.

Once upon a time this had been a Japanese Air Force base, I was sure of it. And I had a good hunch that it was the base from which Colonel Aki Shintu had commanded.

Another thing struck me as we approached the aircraft. If they had wanted me dead, they could have easily killed me long before this. A sniper almost anywhere in the crowds of Tokyo would have done the job, just as the man outside the morgue, or these two, could have killed me.

But it seemed that after the first couple of attempts on my life they had given up any serious try, contenting themselves with merely following me around. Now they had told Taffy they only wanted to talk to me, and these two men had brought us out here without tying us up or blindfolding us.

This was making less and less sense.

The Mercedes pulled up and stopped alongside the DC3, and the man who had frisked me let us out of the car.

"General Shintu is awaiting you, please," he said, indicating the open door of the plane.

"A general now?" I said, smiling.

The man bowed, but said nothing more. He got back in the car and they took off the way we had come.

There was no one on the runway, and I could not see

up into the cockpit of the airplane. Obviously someone was there manning the controls, but at this point we were apparently on our own. I wondered one last time if I was being a fool for going along with them, but then I shrugged. It was the quickest way I knew of getting to the heart of this thing.

I helped Taffy aboard, closing and dogging the door behind us. When she was strapped in her seat, I went forward to tell whoever was flying that we were ready, but as I tried the locked door to the cockpit, the plane surged forward with a roar of the engines and suddenly we were bumping down the runway.

I quickly made it back to my seat next to Taffy's, strapped myself in, and we were airborne.

All the windows in the passenger section of the plane were painted black, so I had absolutely no idea where we were heading, or even the direction we were flying.

During the trip, which lasted less than half an hour, Taffy sat rigidly on her seat, and did not say a word. She was frightened, I supposed, and I felt like a heel once again for ever doubting her. And yet, I still could not bring myself to belief Kazuka was the leak.

I was still pondering that dilemma when the plane began to sink down for its landing, and Taffy gripped the arm of her seat, turning her knuckles white.

A few minutes later, we were on the ground bumping along what was apparently another grass strip, and then we stopped.

By the time Taffy and I were out of our seats, the side door was open and two men armed with automatic weapons entered, motioning us outside to a pair of waiting Jeeps. Taffy was directed into one of the Jeeps which immediately took off down the side of the runway toward a group of Quonset huts in the distance, while I piled into the other and was driven in the opposite direction toward a group of larger, more permanent buildings.

As we drove, with one of my guards keeping the deadly automatic weapon trained on me, I wondered briefly if I would ever see Taffy again—or anyone else for that matter. But then my mind moved on to the more important question of where we were.

Off the end of the runway behind us, past a long row of light airplanes, I could see the ocean and smell its fresh breeze. The dawn was just coming up and from the direction of the sun, I figured we were somewhere west of Honshu, probably out in the straits between Japan and Korea. That was not a very comforting thought. If we were on an island that far from Japan, our only means of escape would be one of the airplanes or possibly a boat.

The Jeep I was in pulled up at one of the larger buildings and I was ordered inside. Before I entered the door, I noticed that all of the windows in the three story barracks had bars on them. I was going to jail. But for how long? And what would happen when they let me out, if ever they did?

CHAPTER FOURTEEN

I don't like being locked up, I never have. I suppose it is a slight claustrophobia, but this time I did not have long to wait.

Barely two hours after my guards had locked me in a tiny room completely devoid of any furnishings, they returned for me, marching me out of the building and into the bright morning sun, but not before I had caught a glimpse of the other people in their cells. Most of them were old, and if every cell contained one person, this building alone could have housed more than a hundred of them.

What had they done against this Aki Shintu, I wondered? And how long had they been kept prisoner?

I had very little time to ponder that question before I was marched around the building and to the edge of a large parade ground filled with what I estimated to be at least two hundred men clad in white kimonos. They all stood at rigid attention, eyes forward toward a reviewing stand.

Tied around their heads was the same kind of prayer shawl I had taken from at least five men so far. I had indeed struck the jackpot. Dealing with one of these fanatics at a time was bad enough, but now I was in the middle of a couple of hundred of them.

A few minutes later an incredibly old man shuffled his way from a low cement block building behind the reviewing stand and climbed carefully up the stairs so that he towered over the assembly. He, too, wore a white kimono, but on the front of his was emblazoned a bright orange Rising Sun—the symbol of the Japanese empire during the war.

No doubt this was the man I had come to see. Aki Shintu, once a colonel and now apparently a self-styled general.

The men, all of them very young, were completely silent as they stood absolutely rigid. When the old man spoke, his voice was surprisingly strong, and it easily carried to where I stood with my guard.

His words seemed to be in the form of some kind of prayer for the greater glory of Japan, its youth and its ancestors. He told the men that the world would never forget what they were about to do, and would remember them as heroes for the destiny of Japan.

Suddenly he was finished, and in unison all two hundred of the Kamikaze warriors raised both arms over their head in salute, and screamed: "Banzai! Banzai! Banzai!"

As the men broke ranks and moved off the parade ground, my guard brought me past the reviewing stand into the cement block building where the old man had retreated.

Taffy was seated forlornly in a chair along one wall near the door which led to the back of the building. When I came in she looked up and nodded at me.

"Where did they take you, Nick?" she said, her voice strangely restrained.

"To a cell," I said, coming across the room to her. "How about you?"

"My mother died this morning," she said, lowering her head.

"They killed her?"

She shook her head. "No, Nick. She was old, and she just died."

I was about to ask her how long she had been sitting here, when the door opened and the old man beckoned us inside.

Taffy got up and we went in and sat down in chairs by a large desk, our guard taking up his position by the door. The old man slowly took his seat behind the desk, and when he was finally settled he looked up at me and smiled.

"Mr. Nick Carter, I'm pleased finally to meet you," he said.

"General Shintu, is it?" I said, trying to match the man's calmness. Something sure as hell was wrong here; I could feel it thick in the air. It was as if I was being toyed with by someone who had nothing to fear from me. I knew that I could disarm my guard and kill the old man in less than ten seconds, and yet something held me back.

"That is correct, although my official rank from the war remains Colonel."

I said nothing. It was his show, and I would let him run it, for now.

"I can see that there are many questions in your mind. The first of which is why were you brought here unharmed."

I nodded. It would do for starters.

"You may not believe this, Mr. Carter, but we are not murderers except in the line of duty. Military duty."

I scoffed and was about to protest, but the old man held up a thin, grizzled hand for my silence. I sat back in my seat. There would be no arguing with this man, I knew. He had the shine in his eyes that has always been the common denominator in any fanatic's makeup. He was completely dedicated to his beliefs.

The old man looked out the window at the empty parade ground for a long moment, finally shaking his head sadly and then turning back to me. Through all of this Taffy had not moved a muscle, as she stared straight ahead at him, and for a moment she too seemed to have the same look of dedication as Shintu. I hoped she was not going to try anything foolish. But then the old man was speaking.

"I will begin from the beginning," he said, "and then our mission will become quite clear to you."

I said nothing.

"We are aware that during the past few days you and

Miss Nashima have engaged in a number of lengthy conversations about Japan and the Japanese spirit. So now it should go without saying that you are at least aware of my people's dedication to the past. To our ancestors, if you will. And to honor."

My estimation of this man and his organization went up still another notch. Taffy's apartment, and perhaps her uncle's house as well, had been bugged. It was frighteningly efficient.

"On August sixth of 1945, one of your American bombers dropped a relatively small thermonuclear device on the city of Hiroshima. Half the population was wiped out and nearly ninety percent of its structures were completely destroyed.

"It was an inhuman act, far worse than any of the atrocities your propoganda ministry told the world we had committed. Innocent men, women and children were needlessly slaughtered."

"It ended the war," I said softly. "It may even have saved the lives of a million people or more."

"It did not end the war." Shintu spat out the words, his calm features breaking into an angry glare. "It only stopped the organized resistance against your kind."

"And you are still fighting the war," I offered.

"Indeed," Shintu said, "but now it will come to an end."

A chill played up my back, and I was suddenly very wary of this man. What was going to happen next? What could he possibly do? And why?

"Of course, we do not expect to conquer the world . . . but before I get to that I will tell you the reason behind all of this." His voice and manner were much calmer now. "My grandmother, mother, three sisters, wife and two children all moved to Hiroshima in July of 1945. They wanted to be close to me where I commanded my squadron. And I was happy for them to be near me. They died three days after the atomic bombing. It would have been merciful for them to be like the many others who were vaporized instantly in the blast, but they lived on in unbelievable agony for seventy-two hours. I finally had them shot, to put them to rest."

I closed my eyes. Perhaps if I had been in Shintu's shoes, I would now be doing the same thing. I don't know for sure. But I was certain that he was a very dangerous man because he had been planning this for thirty years.

I looked up after a moment. "Warnings were given," I said evenly.

"Who could have believed such propoganda, and what rational man could have guessed the inhumanity of the Allies."

It was like a switch in my mind. All the phone calls Owen had made over the world to AXE contacts. They were contacts in the Allied countries of the war. Germany, Italy and Japan were the Axis, and had nothing to do with the bombing.

I blurted out my next thought. "You mean to say you're going to exact retribution from the entire world? From every country that was allied with the United States?"

"That is correct," Shintu said. "And my compliments on your quick mind. Would you care to finish your thoughts?"

I glanced toward the window and tried to think. Somehow this all fit together with the four air crashes that had occurred over the past few months. Then it hit me, and I turned back to the old man.

"All those young men out there on the parade ground this morning—they were pilots?" I asked.

Shintu nodded.

"They are going to leave here and take commercial flights to every major city in the world—except of course for cities in Germany, Italy and here in Japan."

"Continue," Shintu said smiling.

"Just before they land, your people will take over the aircraft and crash them."

"But crash them into major population areas, financial

institutions, government capitol buildings, and any place else where we can inflict the maximum damage. Only a small payment in return for the immeasurable suffering."

"My God, you're nuts," I said. I had to get out of here right now and warn Hawk. Somehow he would have to alert every airline in the world before it was too late. An almost impossible task.

I rose abruptly, causing both Shintu and the guard to start. Strolling carefully to the window I glanced out and noted there was a Jeep parked in front with no one guarding it.

"How did Owen Nashima get wind of your scheme?" I said at last, facing him with my arms crossed.

"There were people loyal to my cause living in the cities to be hit," he said. "I advised them to evacuate in order to avoid being accidentally injured, and Nashima heard about it through his contacts."

"So you killed him," I said.

"He took his toll of my men before I decided he had to be eliminated."

Like hell he did, I thought. The old man was crazy if he believed his plan would cause pain to those responsible for the atomic bombing of Japan. He would be killing innocent people, just like the atomic bomb did, yet he could not see the error in his logic, as twisted as his reason must have been.

"There's one more thing I'd like to know," I said, stepping away from the window and walking between the desk and the guard.

"What?" Shintu said.

I was five feet from the unsuspecting guard when I drew my knee up quickly, spun on my right foot and kicked the gun from his hands. Before he could react, I had followed through my spin and kicked him hard in the stomach.

A chop to the neck put him out cold and I stood before Aki Shintu with the automatic rifle in my hands.

"Now we'll see about getting you to call off this sense-less scheme," I said, breathing heavily.

Shintu sat peacefully and gazed up at me without any trace of fear on his face. "That is impossible. My men have their plans committed to memory and no longer need my leadership. You cannot stop them—not all of them—and within twenty-four hours they will have completed their missions."

I put the rifle to the old man's throat. "I want you to give me the flights you plan to hijack."

He did not bat an eyelash. "I have served my purpose and am prepared to die."

The plan was already in motion. I had not figured it would begin so soon, although I knew it was on the verge of happening. The question now was how to stop it. But with just Taffy—who seemed to be in pretty bad shape—and myself against two hundred dedicated fanatics, the odds were not good, although I did have a hunch that might upset Shintu's plans if I could get out of here. But first I needed some more information.

I turned to Taffy. We're going to make a run for it," I said, and I nodded toward Shintu. "We'll take him as hostage. Do you think you can drive the Jeep?"

She looked fearfully at Shintu and then up at me, and she nodded.

"We'll have to move fast," I said. "We'll have the element of surprise for the first couple of minutes, but if we don't make it to the plane by then we'll be in trouble. Do you want to try?"

She nodded uncertainly, and I flashed her a smile.

"We'll make an AXE agent out of you yet," I said, and then I dragged Shintu to his feet, and pushed him toward the door.

I tightened my grip around his chest and pressed the end of the rifle hard against his throat. I had a feeling that despite what he had told me he was not like his dedicated followers. No. I did not think Shintu was ready to die just yet.

Taffy opened the door and we moved into the empty waiting room. At the outside door, Taffy peeked outside, and then turned back to me.

"There are two guards with weapons about fifty yards away. No one is at the Jeep."

"Let's give it a try," I said.

Taffy opened the door all the way, and we hurried the few feet to the Jeep. I threw the resisting Shintu into the back seat while Taffy jumped in behind the wheel, started the engine and roared off across the parade ground in the direction of the airstrip.

I looked back as the two guards suddenly came alert, raised their automatic rifles in our direction, but then held back. The back of Shintu's head was clearly visible from where they were aiming, and evidently they did not want to hit their leader.

I pulled the automatic rifle around, and sprayed their area, sending them scrambling for cover. With any luck we would be able to make it all the way to the aircraft parking area without anyone firing on us because of Shintu.

As we rounded the corner by one of the barracks and headed down the bumpy road toward the airstrip in the distance, we passed three Jeeps and one open red truck parked side by side. No one fired on us as we passed, but moments later dozens of men were climbing aboard the vehicles. They would be coming after us very soon, I was sure.

I took careful aim with the automatic and before we were out of range, I had managed to riddle the tires of all four vehicles, stopping, at least for the moment, our pursuers.

In less than five minutes we burst onto the airstrip, and Taffy headed toward where the line of aircraft were parked. I had expected the most trouble here, but when we pulled up alongside the DC3, the area was deserted. Evidently our escape had not been expected.

We climbed out of the Jeep, Shintu still struggling

against my grasp, and Taffy quickly clambered aboard the plane. A moment later she reappeared at the door.

"There's no one in here," she said. "Shall I start the engines?"

"Yes?" I said surprised. I hadn't the slightest idea that she knew the controls of the DC3. The plane was not the most sophisticated aircraft around, but it did require an experienced pilot to even make sense out of the instrument panel. I wondered briefly where she learned to fly and why she had not mentioned it before.

Sintu and I started toward the boarding ladder, when a Jeep burst onto the end of the runway, and screamed toward us.

I shoved the old man toward the ladder, but as he took the first step up, he twisted suddenly and with a strength I didn't believe possible for a man his age, he freed himself from my grasp and kneed me forcefully in the groin.

My reflexes saved me from the brunt of his unexpected attack, but a flash of nausea swept through my stomach for an instant, giving him time to break free. By the time I straightened up he was ten feet away and sprinting toward his men, who were halfway down the runway and taking aim in my direction.

I shot from the hip with the automatic rifle as I ran toward Shintu. But now the Jeep was too close, and I had to dodge and roll to avoid their fire. Bullets tore into the turf around my head as I aimed again, hitting two of the three men in the Jeep which had pulled up less than a hundred feet away.

As I swung toward the third man a dull click told me my gun had jammed, and I jumped to my feet trying vainly to work the ejection slide back into position.

The delay gave the man enough time to jump from the Jeep and head in a run toward me.

Shintu, who had stopped to one side of the Jeep, shouted, "Take him alive."

One of the DC3's engines roared to life at that moment, but I knew that I could not make it inside before being pulled down by the onrushing Kamikaze warrior. I stood midway between the plane and the man, took a deep breath and raised the rifle above my head like a club.

The man put up his arms to ward off the blow as he closed on me, but at the last instant I stepped to the side and brought the rifle down and around taking a full, solid swing with it like a baseball bat.

The butt of the rifle caught the man squarely on the chin, breaking his jaw as well as the wooden rifle stock. He straightened up with the blow, and then fell hard, blood spurting from the torn, mangled flesh of his face that was now nothing more than pulp.

It had felt a little crude, but very American, and I'm sure if Babe Ruth had been around to witness my home run he would have been proud.

I turned in Shintu's direction, but found that he was running for the thick bushes a few hundred feet away.

I had taken no more than three steps after him when the sound of several trucks made me stop and head back to the plane. I could not hold off any more men, and was glad to see the second engine turn over and spin to life as I scrambled up the boarding ladder and pulled it into the plane with me. A moment later I had the door shut and dogged.

I rushed up to the cockpit and slid into the pilot's seat as Taffy moved across to the right hand seat. Although I had not flown a DC3 for a number of years, the controls were familiar to me, and I firewalled the throttles and pitch controls as I released the brakes and we were bumping along the runway as the first of the trucks pulled onto the grass strip three thousand feet away.

A short distance down the runway I managed to get the tail up off the ground, and we rapidly picked up speed, but the three trucks now on the runway showed no signs of veering off. They were going to ram us head on to stop us from taking off.

At the last possible moment, I bled in a little flaps and

hauled back on the control wheel and the DC3 leaped
into the air over the trucks, bouncing once on the ground
behind them and then we were airborne.

A few bullets tore into the side of the fuselage, but
soon we were out of range, and were humming northward
over bluegreen waves on our way back to Honshu, and, I
hoped, reinforcements to stop Shintu's insane plan.

CHAPTER FIFTEEN

"We read you, DC3, at four thousand feet on heading zero-one-five. What is your identification, please?"

"No numbers and no flight plan, Kagoshima Control," I said into the microphone. "We're about twenty miles out on a long final. Requesting an emergency landing with police standby."

There was a pause of about a half a minute, then the cabin radio crackled again. "DC3, you're cleared for a straight-in landing on seven. Barometer is two-niner-niner-seven, winds are ten knots from two-four-zero, emergency crews standing by."

"Roger, Kagoshima Control," I said and I put away the mike as I cut back on the throttles. The aircraft began to sink gently as its speed bled off, and a few minutes later the runway came into view as a narrow, long ribbon of concrete directly ahead of us. A big number seven was painted on our end, and already I could see the bright red emergency trucks pulling alongside the runway awaiting our arrival.

At one thousand feet and a little less than two miles from the runway, I put in about twenty degrees of flaps and the ancient aircraft shuddered as it slowed down to final landing speed.

Soon the grass on either side of the runway was rushing past us in a blur and then our wheels bumped once, and gently twice and we were on the ground. Not bad, I told myself, for someone who hasn't flown anything this big for several years.

The control tower guided us along the maze of taxiways toward the maintenance hangers near the main terminal. Evidently they wanted us away from the normal commercial traffic areas.

There were half a dozen armed airport guards and city policemen waiting uneasily for us at the foot of the boarding ladder as Taffy and I stepped to the ground. They looked expectantly up at the door.

"We're the only ones," I said to the police captain, who seemed to be the man in charge.

"Who the hell are you?" he shouted. "And what the hell are you doing flying an unmarked aircraft?"

"Nick Carstens," I said. "I'm with the Amalgamated Press. And we've got some big trouble."

The captain hesitated a moment, evidently unsure of what to say to me.

"I have to make a very important call to Washington, D.C.," I announced. "I'd like your people to guard this plane and I'd like for you to be with me when I make that call."

The captain came out of his momentary daze, "The plane will be impounded," he snapped. "And I will most certainly be with you when you make that call—and it had better be a good one," he added menacingly.

He commanded the airport security men to search the airplane and allow no one in or out of the area under any circumstances. Then, he and three of his metropolitan police officers went with Taffy and me into the maintenance hanger office where I was shown the telephone.

It took almost twenty minutes to complete the connection with our Washington emergency number, and suddenly David Hawk was on the line. I quickly briefed him on the entire story, including my discussion with Aki Shintu.

"I have a pretty fair idea of what cities will be hit," I said. "But not what flights will be hijacked, nor exactly when all of this will take place, although Shintu said it would be over in twenty-four hours."

"What do you want from this end?" Hawk said gruffly, his voice faint on the long-distance lines.

"Our only chance at this point," I shouted into the phone, "will be catching Shintu and his people before they desert the island base. Otherwise I don't know if they can be stopped in time."

The line was silent for a moment, until Hawk came on again. "Sit tight where you are Nick. I'm going to pull the strings here through the President himself. I'll get back to you shortly."

"Yes, sir," I said, and I hung up after giving him my location and telephone number.

"What the hell is going on here?" the captain exploded when I turned to him.

"You heard what I told my boss," I said, but the cop was turning red in the face, and seemed almost ready to burst a blood vessel.

"You don't expect me to swallow that story, do you?" he said through clenched teeth.

I shook my head. "Doesn't matter. If you'll just wait here a few minutes, you'll get your answer when my boss, and probably yours, call back."

I hoped that Hawk would be quick about his connections, because I did not think I would be able to stall this captain off much longer. And if Taffy and I were arrested, it would take too long to straighten everything out in time for us to make it back to Shintu's island and stop them.

Perhaps it was already too late.

Fifteen minutes later Hawk called back on an international conference line which included police and Air Guard authorities here in Japan. The captain and I both listened, sharing the receiver, while Hawk briefed them all, and secured their cooperation in a police action attempt to capture Shintu's island stronghold.

With the proper authorization behind him and the full story explained, the captain turned out to be an aggressive, agreeable man who decided quickly to lead the contingency force of Kagoshima police himself.

Two hours later Taffy and I were airborne again in the

DC3, leading three other large airplanes full of police back to the island. I had carefully recorded our headings back to the mainland, so retracing our path was not difficult. When we reached the island, however, there was no trace of life. The long line of aircraft I had seen earlier parked along the side of the runway was gone, and only a number of Jeeps and trucks lined the runway.

I silently cursed my own stupidity. I should have destroyed the aircraft when I had the chance, but now ... now it was too late.

I clambered down the boarding ladder, and rushed to the Jeeps, finding the ignition keys missing, but no other attempt at disabling the vehicles had been made. They must have known we were coming back, and had taken the keys with them to slow us down.

"They're all gone," Taffy said as she joined me, watching as I found a piece of bare wire in the floorboard of the Jeep and hot-wired the ignition.

The other airplanes had landed, and the police forces were scrambling out and gathering around the other vehicles. I shouted at the captain to have his men hot-wire the ignitions, and follow us.

"There's nothing left here, Nick," Taffy said. "Why go back to the compound?"

"There has to be some kind of clue, or records or something back there," I said as I pulled Taffy into the Jeep. "They left in a hurry but they took the ignition keys with them. They knew we were coming back and they wanted to slow us down looking around. That means they might have left something behind. Something that could help us."

I slammed the Jeep in gear and roared off down the runway, my foot to the floorboards, toward the compound as some of the other vehicles struggled to life and a few of them started after us.

It was a thin hope, I had to admit to myself. But there wasn't too much left for us. Maybe Shintu had been right. Maybe it was too late to stop his mission. Notifying all the airlines in the world would be a mammoth, perhaps even impossible task, in the time remaining, but it would be the only thing we had left unless we found something here.

We pulled up on the deserted parade ground. Absolutely nothing but the empty buildings remained. Aki Shintu and all of his men had gone, leaving nothing behind but their vehicles on the flightline.

A quick inspection of the offices and men's quarters turned up nothing, and ten minutes later we were at the barracks prison on the opposite side of the compound where the police broke down all the locked doors, releasing the more than one hundred prisoners.

Without exception all of the people were elderly, and most of them seemed to be in a dazed condition, not able to do much talking. They had probably been drugged just before Shintu and his men left, so that even when we did release them they would not be of much help to us.

But as the confusion began to clear, with the Kagoshima police transporting them carefully back to the waiting airplanes, several of them managed to pass on the information that they were relatives of the men who had been at this base for more than a year.

And all of them who could talk coherently begged for us to stop Shintu and his mad scheme before it was too late.

Evidently Shintu had not been able to bring himself to kill these old people, although killing them would have been the safest course of action for him to take. It was his Japanese spirit, as he had called it, of respect for elders that had held him back despite his fanatical devotion to his plan.

About an hour later most of the old people had been transported to the aircraft, and I was about ready to leave with Taffy when the Kagoshima Police captain stopped by our Jeep. "A lot of these people here need medical attention," he said. "We'll be taking them directly to Tokyo where there are better facilities."

"All right," I nodded tiredly, trying to make my mind work. There had to be some kind of a solution here. Something I could suggest to Hawk when we got back. Time was running out.

"There is one thing, though," the captain said, breaking into my thoughts. "Thought you might want to know about it."

I was alert now. "What is it?"

"We've got an old man back here—must be close to a hundred—who keeps repeating his own name. Nagao Shintu. Said he has something to tell us. . . ."

I started to get out of the Jeep, interrupting him. "Where is he?" I snapped.

"Hold on," the captain said. "He's unconscious now. But we loaded him on your plane with one of the medical people. Thought you might like to talk to him on the way back, if he regains consciousness."

It took another full four for us to refuel the aircraft from the undamaged fuel depot at one end of the runway, and get back into the air. In addition to the medical man on board our DC3, the captain had assigned us a police pilot, leaving me free to watch over the old man.

Halfway to Tokyo he finally regained consciousness, but at first I could not make much sense of his babbling. Suddenly his mind cleared when I asked him if he was Aki Shintu's brother. He smiled.

"I am ten years older than he," he croaked slowly as if each word was an effort.

He wore a faded purple kimono and sandals, and had the same triangular face, drooping mustache and tuft of hair around a bald head that his brother had. His eyes, though watery and weak, did not have the glint of madness that I had seen in Aki Shintu's.

"Why were you placed in the cell?" I asked.

"I tried to dissuade Aki from his venture. He put me there to keep me from notifying the authorities. I would have, too." He smiled again. "That was the main reason, but he also did not like the manner in which I reminded him that his plan was lunatic. For years I told him he was concentrating on an unhealthy memory and should put it away, but he only called me a traitor."

"How long has he been working on this?" I asked.

"Five years. He talked with many people and must have kept lists of prospective volunteers. But he only brought them together during the last year. That is, when he found the island with its runway." The old man coughed and could not talk for a long moment.

"How did you get onto the island?"

"He took me there to show me his camp. He was very proud of it; strutting over the grounds and telling me how everyone would admire him when he righted the wrong done by the Allies."

Shintu suddenly became serious. "He was a rich man. Air transport business after the war under an assumed name. Financed this entire thing himself. His planes, too. All he had to do was keep an eye out for fanatical youngsters to recruit for the greater glory of our country."

"I've heard that phrase before," I smiled grimly.

"I told him what I thought when I first saw the camp. I told him he was disturbed, and should give up his crazy idea."

"And he never let you leave the island after that?"

He nodded. "But he only put me in the cell for the last few weeks to keep me out of the way. I was a pest, you know."

I smiled at the pluck he still possessed. "I bet you were."

"But there has to be a way to stop him. You must. But how can one swat a swarm of flies with one hand?"

Taffy had been crouching behind me through the interview, and now she spoke up. "We have to find Aki Shintu," she said. "Then maybe we'll be able to stop this."

I looked over my shoulder at the serious expression on her face, but said nothing.

"Nick, I think I might have an idea where he is right now," she said, excitement creeping into her voice.

She had my interest now. "Go on," I urged.

"He's probably going to be on one of the Stateside planes out of Tokyo," she said.

I couldn't see what she was driving at, or how she was arriving at her conclusions. She read the expression on my face.

"Don't you see, Nick, since the U.S. made the atomic bomb and dropped it on Hiroshima, he would have to be the one to hijack the Stateside plane."

"But which one?" I said, coming to my feet. She was right, I could feel it. But there would be dozens of U.S. cities as targets.

"Washington, D.C.," she said.

It all came clear suddenly, and for a moment I felt like a fool. Where had my mind been? The conclusion was logical I nodded, and she continued.

"But if my guess is right, you're going to want to use him to stop the others from attacking, so we'll have to try and take him alive. Getting the police in on this now would probably end in a fight, and there would be nothing to stop the others."

Everything she was saying was correct. So now, once again, it was up to me . . . or rather us, and we probably didn't have much time.

I jumped up and made my way forward to the cockpit, and slid into the co-pilot's seat. I had to shout over the noise of the engines.

"How long before we arrive at Tokyo International?" I asked.

"About an hour," he said, leaning slightly in my direction.

"Can you raise the tower from here?" I shouted.

The pilot nodded. "I think so," he said.

"I want the departure times of all aircraft leaving for Washington, D.C., within the next six hours," I said.

The pilot nodded again, then turned to his radio. He switched to the proper frequency and then began speaking into the microphone. I could not hear what he was saying because of the engine noise, but after a few moments he pushed back the headphones he was using and turned to me.

"They'll have the information for us in about ten minutes," he said.

I waited in the cockpit until I had my answer from the Tokyo tower, and then I went to the back of the plane to Taffy. It was going to be close. The first 747 jumbo jet on a non-stop flight to Washington would be leaving about fifteen minutes after our estimated arrival time. And there was no way we could get there any faster. The pilot assured me he had been pushing the ancient craft to its limit all along, and could nurse no more speed from it.

I had given specific instructions to the tower—on local Japanese authority worked out for me by Hawk—not to allow the 747 to take off before we arrived and boarded it. But I also cautioned the tower not to make it obvious that the plane was being delayed because of us.

"There's only one plane leaving non-stop for Washington and we'll just make it," I told Taffy as I crouched down beside her and the old man.

"What then?" Taffy said.

I hesitated. "Capture him," I said. "Use him to stop his men."

She said nothing, but the look of deep concern and fright was back into her face, as it had been when we were in Aki Shintu's office.

I turned to the old man. "When did your brothers begin bringing the prisoners to the island?" I asked.

"Most of them came in the last few months," he said.

"Did he seem to enjoy having them there?" It was a seemingly innocuous question, but one of vital importance for me if my hastily conceived plan was going to work.

The old man managed a laugh. "No," he said. "It caused great embarrassment to him. He had to keep the pilots' family members quiet. Many of them knew about his scheme and threatened to call the police. The only way he could prevent that was to imprison them, but he felt very bad for putting members of families, especially the elders, in cells. Family should not be mistreated."

I thought that over for a long moment, then turned to Taffy. "That just might be it," I said, showing more confidence than I felt. "We might be able to stop him after all."

CHAPTER SIXTEEN

The desk attendant at the flight gate was just locking the chain in place when Taffy and I ran up and waved our tickets at him. The last of the waiting passengers were shuffling slowly through a door beside a window, the giant 747 crouching outside like a tamed beast.

"Two more," I said, laying the tickets on the desk. We had taken the time to arrange for ordinary coach accomodations in order not to raise suspicions at the gate. So far everything had gone smoothly. Almost too smoothly.

"Where would you like to sit?" the young man said pleasantly.

I glanced out the window and saw that the boarding ramp was connected to the rear door of the aircraft. "Put us near the back of the plane," I said. That way we would not have to walk past too many people to reach our seats. With any luck at all Shintu and his men would not notice our arrival.

The attendant nodded and stamped our tickets, then placed stickers on them to indicate the seats. Unhooking the chain, he welcomed us through and sent us to the boarding tunnel, where we rushed to the plane.

A stewardess swung the large door shut after we entered, sealing us into the interior of the aircraft, a gray and white cave filled with muted talk and suddenly the vibrations of jet engines starting. A world unto itself, the gigantic cigar-shaped cabin might have been a coffin unto itself as well, unless we were successful.

"Take the inside seat," I said to Taffy when we found our row. "I'll take the aisle seat." While Taffy was sitting down I stood in the aisle and scanned as far forward as I could. Seeing no one who resembled Shintu, I carefully

154

made my way forward and paused near the stairway which led to the First Class cocktail lounge upstairs.

I carefully studied the backs of the heads sticking above the seats, and was about to give up and move further forward, when a shiny distant head caught my attention.

Shintu was seated near the front of the Tourist Class cabin in an aisle seat, and wearing a gray suit. The bald head and tuft of white hair was unmistakable. Beside him, in the two seats closer to the window, I saw the shiny dark hair of young Oriental men who would be the weapons man and the pilot for this particular suicide squad.

I stepped back to avoid being seen should they glance around. They were seated in a perfect position, from my point of view, because if they stepped out into the aisle on their way to the cockpit door, they would come into my line of fire.

I ducked back down the aisle and slipped into the seat next to Taffy just as the stewardess came our way to ask me to sit down and buckle my seatbelt. The jet was backing out of its berth, and when the stewardess saw that I was finally strapped in, she retreated to the rear to dictate into the ship's loudspeaker system the emergency instructions required by international law before every flight.

"They're near the front," I said to Taffy. "We'll make our move as soon as the plane is at altitude."

Taffy nodded and I could see that she was nervous.

"They might try to shoot it out here and then escape if we attempted to stop them. But at altitude, over the ocean, I don't think they'll risk it. It would ruin everything for them."

Fortunately, airport security had been notified of our special status so I did not have to go through the normal security precautions, which would have relieved me of any weapons.

Within minutes, the plane was off the ground, the landing gear had come up, and we were heading out across the ocean for the long trip halfway around the world. Long before we arrived, however, I hoped to have this entire case wrapped up . . . safely.

As soon as the seatbelt and no-smoking signs were shut off and the plane had leveled off, the stewardesses made their drink runs. When they had disappeared into the galleys at the rear I turned to Taffy.

"It's just about time. . . ," I started, but Taffy deftly slipped her hand across my stomach and pulled my gun out of its holster. The Tokyo police gave me a Lugar to replace confiscated Wilhelmina.

She cocked it and leveled the muzzle at my stomach, her lips fixed in a determined frown.

I stared at her for several long seconds, not able to speak because of the confusion in my mind. But then it was as if the fog lifted one last time, and things began to make some sense to me, as several unlikely coincidences in the past week fell into place in a single pattern of betrayal. The suicide squads who seemed to know my every move. The times Taffy had interfered with me, almost costing me my life. They were mistakes all right, but mistakes for the wrong side in not managing to kill me.

"You're one of them," I said simply.

Her face was a blank, but she nodded.

I felt strange, as if wrenched from one world and thrust painfully into a new one and forced to deal with emotions turned upside-down. I wanted to ask her why, but I could detect no trace of the softness in her face. Whatever she felt for me was hidden behind a mask I could not penetrate. Nor could I gauge the depth of her committment to Shintu's Kamikaze Corps.

She stared at me as I studied her eyes and wondered what to say. The next move was hers, and yet she seemed to hesitate as if letting me have time for an opening.

"Well?" I said finally.

"You don't have long to live," she said.

I really did not believe she had it in her to kill me, yet I realized I never really knew Taffy as well as I thought

I did. Maybe she was capable of this. Maybe she was highly capable.

"You can't be serious," I said as flippantly as possible.

"I am," she said, and there was no change in the coldness of her eyes.

"Aki Shintu is mad. He's emotionally unstable. You heard his brother," I said. "I can't believe you be be naïve enough to follow him."

Her eyes hardened. "He was correct. All you Americans are decadent. You do not understand the higher truth."

"Spoken like a true fanatic," I snapped. "You mean you agree with his idea of revenge for Hiroshima?" My voice was heavy with sarcasm, and she flared at me.

"I had uncles and aunts at Hiroshima. They died there, and I will not forget it."

I was silent for a moment, taking in this new bit of information. I had not known that her relatives, or at least some of them, had died in the bombing. "How did you get involved with Shintu?" I asked, softening my tone.

"Two of my uncles were Kamikaze pilots. The two youngest sons of my mother's parents."

"Did they die?"

"At Luzon," she nodded triumphantly.

Kamikaze uncles for her to look up to. I could not believe they could have molded her character so deeply. "What about your father, and Owen?"

"Those ... pigs." Hatred made her eyes even more hard. "My father deserted us. And Owen was never more to me than a reminder of his father. Neither had any loyalty to his country nor to his family. They brought disgrace on us all."

"Did Owen help you get in with AXE?" I asked.

She nodded. "After my oath of allegiance with Aki Shintu, I was ordered to penetrate my brother's business. At the time we did not know what he was doing, but we suspected he was working for the American government. And it was a good thing for us I did."

"So you fingered your own brother for the kill," I said, hoping to goad her into making a foolish move.

"He was no longer my brother. Besides, it had to be done. It was too late for us to capture him alive. He was heading to the airport. All we could do was get a couple of our people on board that airliner."

"Why wasn't I killed earlier?"

She showed the slightest trace of a smile, almost a hint of admiration. "We tried, but you were too good. We wanted to make it look like an accident at first." She paused for a moment and looked around as a stewardess came up the aisle with a tray of drinks.

"If you try to signal to her, I'll kill you immediately," she said, drawing the Luger close to her own stomach, rendering it invisible from the aisle.

I glanced up at the stewardess but said nothing, and as she moved away, Taffy continued.

"We didn't know how much you had discovered about us, and it seemed like a poor idea to expend any more of our troops in the attempt to kill you. We needed them for the attack. So we let you come in close and then took you prisoner." She smiled bitterly. "Our master thought it would be fitting for you to die on the plane with us. But when you escaped I thought all was lost, until I realized how simple it would be to maneuver you aboard."

"For the greater glory of Japan," I said.

She smiled. "Our master knows we are sitting here. While you were busy with the police at Kagoshima I telephoned him at our Tokyo contact number. He told me what to do. Exactly. When I pull the trigger, you will be out of the way and we will take control of this plane." She spoke with a confidence that told me she was going to carry through. And soon.

She moved back and her eyes narrowed slightly in a squint I had seen many times on the faces of gunmen just before they squeeze the trigger.

I threw my left arm upward at the same instant the Luger roared.

The pain of the bullet jolted my entire arm as I lowed through on my swing and knocked the gun to the left before she could fire again. The first shot had caught me in the upper arm and torn through my biceps, but the numbing effect hit me only after I had diverted her aim. Then I winced as pain shot through my arm and I found myself battling with only one good arm.

She knocked my hand upward, but before she could bring the gun down, I chopped her wrist with my right hand and knocked her off balance. A second blow shook the Luger free and sent it over the seat onto the floor, out of sight and out of reach.

I flipped my wrist, pulling a new Hugo (obtained from the police) free from its chamois case, but Taffy was one step ahead of me. She hit my wounded arm forcefully and managed to climb quickly over me into the aisle, before I could recover from the mind-searing pain.

I jumped up, just missing her, as she headed down the aisle in a dead run, to warn Shintu. If she alerted him I would have little hope of overpowering her, Shintu and his two men.

As she moved away from me, a split instant of emotions and memories swept through my mind. She looked so harmless, so frail. Yet she had set Owen—her own brother—up for the kill, and she had almost killed me just now.

Hawk's last words to me aboard the nuclear submarine flashed into mind. "Unconditional termination," he had said.

Owen had been set up as a result of Taffy's AXE information. She had been an AXE cryp for more than a year, learning everything there was to know.

There was no help for it.

I drew the stiletto back and threw it.

The blade was a blur as it flew, and I could not see exactly where it hit before she crumpled silently to the floor.

Other passengers were just beginning to react to the gunshot when I reached down to retrieve my Luger, and by the time I made my way to her side, shouting people were leaning over their seats and craning to see what had happened.

I holstered my gun and knelt over her, lifting her dark hair off her neck, and feeling for a pulse with my good hand. Her heartbeat was slow, but regular, and she was unconscious.

"What's going on?" a heavy faced man with a scowl demanded. His wife peeked timidly past his ample stomach and tried to see Taffy.

The dagger had plunged deeply into her left side near the heart. There was a strong flow of blood, but I dared not move her to see where it had penetrated. I ignored the passengers and motioned for the stewardess running toward us.

"See what you can do for her," I said softly.

She stared at me, and I glanced down to see blood soaking my lower sleeve and beginning to drip on the floor.

"I'm okay," I said, rising and stepping past her.

So far Shintu and his men apparently did not know anything had gone wrong. If they had heard the shot, they must have figured Taffy had been successful and were now waiting for her to join them.

I hurried forward, past the bathrooms by the spiral steps to the lounge, and as I stepped into the forward cabin area Shintu was just coming into the aisle, his back to me. He said something to one of his men, and then turned my way.

For a shocked moment he looked at me, and then dove out of the way, giving his two men free aim at me. I had the Luger out and fired the first shot, dropping one of Shintu's warriors.

As he fell, the second man came out from behind the seat raising a submachinegun. I dropped to my knee and fired three shots which hit him in the stomach, the throat and the forehead. As he jerked back, a pistol shot whacked into the seat next to my head. Shintu.

I ducked into a vacant seat as the passengers all began to scream and shout and a second shot was fired at me, slamming into the seat back next to me.

For several long seconds there were no more shots fired, and I peeked around the edge of my seat into the aisle as the first man I had shot slumped back, a pistol falling from his hand.

Evidently he had been the one doing the shooting, not Shintu. I hurried up the aisle, past the passengers too frightened now to say anything to a wounded man armed with a gun.

When I reached the row I had last seen Shintu duck into, I cautiously peered over the armrest of a seat, and he was there, crouching on the floor, unarmed making little attempt to hide.

I holstered my gun. "It's all over for you now," I said tiredly.

He looked up, then struggled up into his seat and motioned for me to take the seat next to him. "For me, yes," he said. "But not for the others." He smiled serenely.

"Don't be so sure," I said, because it was the only thing I could think of to say at the moment.

CHAPTER SEVENTEEN

David Hawk rose from behind a massive redwood desk as I ushered Aki Sintu into the executive office at San Francisco International Airport to where our flight had been diverted. It was an expensively decorated room with mahogony and redwood furniture, deep carpeting and floor-to-ceiling windows that overlooked the control tower and a spiderweb of runways near the terminal building.

"So this is Colonel Shintu," Hawk said after I had closed the door behind us.

Aki Shintu closed his eyes momentarily and bowed in greeting, then arched his eyebrows in question at Hawk and the two men with him.

"I'm David Hawk," my chief said. "Nick, this is Armstrong of the FCC and Hartstein of the Federal Aviation Administration." He indicated each man with his cigar as he spoke, and I shook hands with them. Shintu stood aloof.

"Sit down," Hawk said, motioning us to chairs. He returned to his padded, high-backed executive chair. "We'd like to ask you a few questions, Colonel," he continued after we had sat down.

Shintu nodded.

"How long have you planned this adventure of yours?" Hawk began.

Shintu glanced disdainfully at the others, and then smiled toward me. "Killmaster Carter knows the details of my Special Attack Corps."

I had to smile at his words. He evidently felt some kind of a bond with me because I, too, was a warrior, while these others were at best merely bureaucratic officials of the U.S. Government.

162

"Is that correct?" Hawk asked, his eyebrow raised as if he was amused with Shintu's admiration of me.

"He kept a diary of his Kamikaze Corps," I said. "It covers his thoughts from day one to the present."

"And you have that diary?"

I nodded. "Yes sir. He was carrying it with him on the flight. I found it after the incident."

Hawk was about to ask for the diary, but I held up my hand.

"We're going to have to do some fast work, sir," I said. "As far as I can figure from what's happened so far, and what Shintu wrote in his diary, all hell would break loose the moment his flight crashed in Washington, D.C., That would have been due to happen in less than two hours."

Hawk nodded. "But before we get started, I just wanted to let you know that Takeha Nashima has been hospitalized. They're operating on her within the next hour."

I nodded silently. I was going to have to do a lot of thinking about her, but now was not the time. Turning back to Shintu, I braced myself for what I hoped would be the final stage of this fight—a fight with a happy outcome.

"I'm curious about an inconsistency concerning your prisoners on the island base," I said.

Shintu's eyes became serious.

"Your brother was one of those prisoners."

He nodded, and I paused for a long moment, bringing my thoughts together.

"Carter, what the hell is this all about?" Hawk blurted.

"Shintu had two hundred hardened, trained Kamikaze pilots in his attack force," I said. "But their families didn't always go along with Shintu's plan." I gazed at the old warrior for a moment. "In fact, many were so opposed that they threatened to notify the police, so Shintu took them prisoner and kept them isolated on his island."

"Only until the attack was carried out, Mister Hawk," Shintu interjected. "Then they were to be released." He looked at me as though he thought I would back him up, but I merely frowned and said nothing to support his statement. I had one last gamble to break his conspiracy, and I now was putting it into operation. It was a psychological gamble that might work if I could handle it just right.

I cleared my throat. "Why did you let your brother live?"

Shintu sat upright in surprise. "What do you mean?"

"I mean why didn't you kill him? He was in your way wasn't he? And hadn't he threatened to go to the authorities?"

"He is my flesh and blood. I would never harm him," Shintu said in indignation.

I listened a moment and then turned to peer out the window for a while, acting as if I did not believe him. Finally I turned back.

"That's not what Taffy Nashima told me on the plane after she was wounded," I lied. "She said the plan was to kill all remaining relatives before the attack if I hadn't forced you to leave prematurely."

"No!" Shintu shouted with a cry that was heavy with anger. He stood up suddenly, quivering with rage. "Family must never be harmed!"

"What about Taffy's brother—Owen Nashima?" I said loudly. "He was cut down in cold blood by your men, and Taffy was the one who set him up. She's the one who knew he had cracked your plan and was going to the States to expose it. In effect, she killed her own brother, not to mention several dozen other Japanese on that aircraft."

"Oshigao Nashima was a traitor to his family and the homeland," Shintu said quietly. He sat back down. "Takeha had disowned him. He was no longer her brother."

"Did Owen's mother feel that way?" I asked.

Shintu was obviously embarrassed and said nothing.

"His mother did not know he was dead, did she," I said, taking a stab in the dark.

He lowered his eyes, but remained mute.

"Taffy could not quite bring herself to tell her mother that her only son was dead for fear of her reaction," I said and I sensed his confusion and now guilt, and pursued him relentlessly.

"In effect, you used your relatives. You didn't care for them at all. You used them like pawns, slapped them into cells if they did not cooperate, and in the end you were prepared to kill them rather than risk exposure of your own fanatical scheme."

Shintu shook his bowed head slowly. "No, Mr. Carter. Family comes first. Absolutely first in my world. There was no plan to harm anyone related to my pilots. Owen Nashima was an extreme case who was dealt with because of his AXE investigations. In fact. . . ." He looked up at me with eyes that implored me to believe him. "In fact, we warned him to give up his work several weeks earlier, but he only used our warnings to learn more about who was in my group and what we were trying to do."

I glanced at Hawk and the other two men, and shook my head slightly. I did not want them to interrupt, not just yet.

"You said you were going to let the relatives go. How? All of you would be dead." I said.

"I have made arrangements on the mainland. In a day or two fishermen will come out and release them."

I changed the subject. "Did your men really know how their families hated the idea of a second generation of Kamikaze pilots?"

"They did not hate the idea," Shintu protested.

But he had hesitated slightly before saying that, and his pause told me everything I needed to know. My plan would work.

"Really?" I continued. "Your diary indicates that you brought your pilots to the island immediately after they pledged themselves to your cause, and that you kept them there for as long as you could. You also wrote that they became unhappy with the isolation so you let them visit the mainland for short periods."

Shintu nodded.

"But you forbade them to visit their families during those trips."

He hesitated.

"It's written in your diary," I said harshly. "I can read it aloud if you wish."

"You are correct," he sighed at last. "I felt I had to isolate them somewhat."

"You let them exchange letters with their families, to keep up their spirits, but you censored those letters," I continued.

He nodded again.

Hawk had become more and more animated as he listened, and when he saw what I had been leading up to, he could no longer contain himself.

"So you really don't know how strong your men's Kamikaze fervor really is, do you?" he said, rising and sitting on the edge of the large desk. "You nurtured their spirit in an isolated psychological environment and didn't want to take any chances they'd back out if their families put pressure on them."

Shintu did not answer, but his downcast eyes betrayed his feeling that Hawk was correct.

Hawk smiled at me with a mixture of triumph and pride. "Good work, Carter," he said, and he turned to the FAA man. "Abe, is it possible to contact all aircraft anywhere in the world? We will have to broadcast a message to the hijacked planes, but we don't know exactly which ones were targeted or where they are at this particular moment."

Hartstein took off his glasses and rubbed the bridge of his nose as he thought for a moment. "All commercial aircraft are in contact with some Air Traffic Control facility at all times. I suppose we could reach them through the ATC net, although nothing like that has ever even been attempted before. Maybe use the emergency frequencies."

He turned to the FCC man. "Can we set up a worldwide network like that, Barny?"

The FCC man frowned as we all turned to him. "I suppose so, but we'd have to do some mighty fancy explaining when it was all over."

"I can handle that," Hawk interceded. "The President has given the green light to anything we come up with here. Let's get it done first and worry about backtracking later."

Hartstein nodded after a long moment. "We can use the control tower here for the operation. We'll tie everything into San Francisco, but we'll have to rush it."

"Then rush it," Hawk snapped. "We'll have our hands full making the message we want to send."

As the two men left the office, Hawk turned to me. "You've been the closest to this Nick. Do you think you can come up with something, and quick?"

"Yes, sir," I said. I turned and glanced at Shintu who seemed to have shrunk somehow into a shell far away from us. And for a moment I almost felt sorry for him. It probably would have been better for him if he had died during an operation in the war, because when the peace had been signed, Shintu had outlived his usefulness to himself. In his own mind, he was already dead, like the kamikaze pilots he had commanded. Only he could not rest, so he had come up with his fanatical scheme. I only hoped that I would be able to come up with something that would work.

Ten hours later, Hawk and I stood in the giant glass cage atop the control tower overlooking the vast airport in San Francisco. It was pitch-black outside, past midnight, and we both sipped coffee and paced anxiously behind the flight controllers huddled over their microphones, their faces ghostly from the faint green of the radar screens in the consoles facing them. The FCC and FAA men had done their jobs well, and every few minutes the murmur of a dozen voices in the tower would cease completely as the flight controllers stopped what they were doing to listen to a ninety second Japanese language broadcast that was being beamed to literally every commercial aircraft in flight in the world.

The message had been fairly simple to come up with once I had come to completely accept what Taffy and Shintu had been telling me all along about Japanese honor.

SHINTU ATTACK CORPS . . . YOUR BROTHERS AND SISTERS HAVE BEEN NOTIFIED OF YOUR KAMIKAZE FLIGHT. THEY EXPRESS THEIR REGRET THAT YOU HAVE CHOSEN TO BRING SHAME AND DISHONOR UPON THE FAMILY, THAT YOU DEFILE YOUR FATHER'S NAME. THEY BESEECH YOU TO RECONSIDER AND ALLOW THEM TO HOLD THEIR HEADS HIGH.

YOUR FATHER BEGS YOU NOT TO FOLLOW THROUGH WITH YOUR PLAN TO KILL INNOCENT PEOPLE AND BRING SHAME ON HIS HEAD. YOUR MASTER AKI SHINTU HAS GIVEN UP, THUS RESTORING HONOR TO HIS FAMILY'S NAME.

YOUR MOTHER THREATENS TO TAKE HER LIFE IF YOU CARRY THROUGH WITH THIS SHAMEFUL ACT. . . .

As we listened, a uniformed official from the airport entered the room and handed Hawk and piece of paper. "From Hartstein, sir," he said.

"Thanks," Hawk replied, glanced at the message and then handed it to me. "The latest tally," he said. "Three crash dives in Europe. Hundreds killed. Twelve planes hijacked, but landed safely."

"Some of them are coming around," I said.

Hawk nodded. "Fifteen accounted for so far." He took

a drink of coffee and threw the half full cup into a waste-basket, then lit a cigar and studied the pattern of blue lights which marked out the crisscross of taxiways leading to the long rows of white runway lights. "But what about the others?" he said half to himself.

Another six hours passed slowly, and dawn was lightening the eastern horizon when we received our last report. It made Hawk break into one of his rare smiles.

"All planes except for three have landed safely. Only three, Nick, out of more than a hundred." He waved the paper at me, and chewed vigorously on his cigar.

I stretched and tried to shake the weariness from my body. "Good," I said, which was all I could think to say. For the past week or so, I had not had much sleep, or any regular meals. It was going to be good to relax for awhile.

"Let's have some breakfast," Hawk said moving toward the door. "We'll get Hartstein and Armstrong to join us. They've been up all night too. And they did a hell of a job."

"What happened to Shintu?" I asked.

The door to the control tower opened at that moment and a messenger handed Hawk another message.

"He's in a safe place now," Hawk said absent-mindedly as he read. His face became blank for a moment, then he frowned and glanced at me.

"Taffy is dead," he said, handing the paper to me. "During open heart surgery two hours ago."

I took the message and continued to stare at Hawk, then handed it back without reading it. I went out the door. Hawk caught up with me as I waited for the elevator to take me downstairs.

"You were under orders, Nick," he said. "Don't wallow in guilt over this. She killed Owen and would have had you too if you hadn't been on your toes. Don't let memories of a different girl cloud your judgment of what she had become."

I looked at him and nodded, and we went down in the

elevator together. In time I would sort it out and have a less emotional view of it all, I was sure of it, but for the time being Japan and Aki Shintu did not mean as much as my memory of a warm, smiling woman.

But Hawk was correct, I supposed. The Taffy I had known five years ago when Owen and I were working together was a different girl from the one who had just died.

When we reached the lower level of the control tower, Hawk and I crossed an open air ramp which led to the terminal. The roar of distant jets filled our ears, and they reminded me of the time I had come here less than two weeks ago to meet Owen, and of the carnage of the crash; the dead strewn across acres of destroyed suburban housing. And I found myself angry at Taffy for taking his friendship away from me.

Hawk opened the door and smiled sadly. "A couple of weeks relaxation won't do you any good this time," he said. "I've got you booked on a flight which leaves here in a couple of hours. Your next mission has begun. You'll be briefed in our branch office. A simple matter really, and when you're done you can take the time off."

I swung my head angrily to say something bitter at him, but stopped when I saw his eyes. I hesitated for a moment, then closed my mouth and walked through the doorway, wondering what would be waiting for me. Sooner or later I would have my vacation, and I knew now where I would spend it—in Tokyo, for that promised dinner and drink with Kazuka Akiyama.

NICK CARTER

"Nick Carter out-Bonds James Bond."
—<u>Buffalo Evening News</u>

Exciting, international espionage adventure with Nick Carter, Killmaster N3 of AXE, the super-secret agency!

☐ THE ULTIMATE CODE 84308-5 $1.50
Nick Carter delivers a decoding machine to Athens—and finds himself in a CIA trap.

☐ BEIRUT INCIDENT 05378-5 $1.50
Killmaster infiltrates the Mafia to stop a new breed of underworld killer.

☐ THE NIGHT OF THE AVENGER 57496-3 $1.50
From Calcutta, to Peking, to Moscow, to Washington, AXE must prevent total war.

☐ THE SIGN OF THE COBRA 76346-4 $1.50
A bizarre religious cult plus a terrifying discovery join forces against N3.

☐ THE GREEN WOLF CONNECTION 30328-5 $1.50
Middle-eastern oil is the name of the game, and the sheiks were masters of terror.

Available wherever paperbacks are sold or use this coupon.

The MS READ-a-thon needs young readers!

Boys and girls between 6 and 14 can join the MS READ-a-thon and help find a cure for Multiple Sclerosis by reading books. And they get two rewards — the enjoyment of reading, and the great feeling that comes from helping others.

Parents and educators: For complete information call your local MS chapter, or call toll-free (800) 243-6000. Or mail the coupon below.

Kids can help, too!